www.chelleblis.com

CHELLE BLISS

USA TODAY BESTSELLING AUTHOR

COPYRIGHT @ 2023 BLISS INK

Publisher © Chelle Bliss April 18th 2023
Edited by Lisa A. Hollett
Proofread by Read By Rose
Cover Design © Chelle Bliss
Dust Jacket Elements © Tanafortuna Art
Cover Photo © Furious Fotog
Cover Model Alex Turner

www.chellebliss.com
CHELLE BLISS
USA TODAY BESTSELLING AUTHOR

CHAPTER 1
FRANCO

"FRANKIE, for fuck's sake. Answer your phone." Jack's voice carries through the shop, echoing from deep under the hood of a late nineties town car.

I'm leaning my elbows on the ancient metal shop desk, sorting through a goddamn mountain of paperwork as though the answer to the meaning of the universe is on one of those purchase orders. The even more ancient desk chair creaks under my weight.

"Frankie!" Jack times his shout to the momentary pause before the bass of the song booming through the speakers kicks up to eardrum-splitting.

"Fuck, man, you want me to find that slip or what?" I yell back.

I've got a one-track mind, and I mean that literally.

You want my attention, you get it. All of it.

You want diagnostics run on a fuel pump, the best cup of coffee you ever had, a night of mind-melting orgasms courtesy of my tongue, or even a lost purchase order found—I can do every one of those things exceptionally well. But only one damned thing at a time.

Finding that piece of paper Jack lost in this mess on the desk will take every shred of patience I have left.

And to be honest, I didn't even hear my phone. I can't believe *he* can hear anything over the hair band he has blaring.

I curse under my breath and try to find the slip of paper that my buddy insists is here—somewhere.

If Jack's parents weren't going through some shit, I would have gotten my ass out from behind the desk and back under one of the dozen cars we have waiting for work, telling him to find the goddamn paperwork himself. But Jack's my oldest friend, this is his shop, and without his mom here to keep the books, he's in way over his head.

"Come on, man. Did you find it?" Jack demands.

I want to tell him to find his own needle in this haystack, but instead, I just hold up a hand and flip him the bird while I shove aside papers of all shapes and sizes.

One problem at a time.

I grab my phone and swipe the screen, and I see not one, not two, but three different messages, all from the same sender.

Mom: Frankie, sweetheart, it's your mother. Can you take a quick break and meet me at Latterature? It's urgent but not life-threatening. Love, Ma

Mom: Franco, honey. It's almost lunch. Do your mother a favor and run down to the bookstore. I won't keep you long. It's very, very important. Love you, sweetheart. Ma

Mom: Son, please, now I'm getting worried. You work five minutes away. Are you coming? Love, your mother Lucia

Three separate text messages composed in full sentences. Each one addressed to me. Each one signed by my mother.

No matter how many times I've explained that she doesn't have to sign her texts, it's a habit she'll never break. And just like when we were kids, Ma escalates the urgency of her texts by switching from *Ma* to *your mother*. And worse, her full name.

"J!" I yell over the music, rolling back on the wheelie chair that normally belongs to Carol, Jack's mom. "I got to run out. You want me to bring back lunch?"

Jack isn't listening or didn't hear me, so I head over to the hood of the town car and press the off button on that damn Hello Kitty speaker.

"Yo!" I shout in the sudden silence. "I'm running to Latterature. You want somethin'?"

Jack shakes his head and rolls his eyes. "My mom made me lunch today, man. I'm sorted."

Even though the marriage stuff going down with his parents is rough, I have to give him shit about it. "What, she pack you a Lunchable and a little note?" I tease.

Jack kicks a work boot at my leg, but intentionally misses. "Fuck off." Then he sighs. "She's staying with me this week. She insists on packing me lunches and making dinners. It's her way of thanking me for letting her crash at my place."

I clap a hand on the hood of the car and nod. "All right, man. So, you're set with your ham sando with the crusts cut off. You want a coffee or something while I'm out?"

"Nah." Jack sniffs and gives me half a grin. "Ma packed my camping thermos. She thinks I spend too much money eating out."

I snort-laugh and almost give him shit for that. Almost.

Yeah, we may be grown men in our late thirties, but if Ma makes it, we eat it. Ma says it, we pay attention.

Hell, I'm about to leave work, thanks to three text messages from my ma, so I don't have much room to give him a hard time about being a mama's boy.

"All right," I say instead and nod. "I'll be back."

I take the love of my life, my Harley-Davidson Road King, through town, waving and nodding at the many people I know along the two-mile drive between the shop and downtown Star Falls.

When I finally reach Main Street, I drive all the way to the farthest end of the strip of quaint storefronts and park right outside the bookstore café.

It isn't even noon yet, so I don't bother stopping by The Body Shop, the tattoo parlor next door. It's Tuesday, which means my little sister, Grace, will be opening the shop, but not until one—and that's if she is on time. Gracie is unpredictable, stubborn, and—more than anything—loves her sleep.

As I pull open the door to Latterature, I'm braced for the string of Christmas bells that normally go off like a wind chime caught in a tornado. But today—nothing. No warning bells, no chimes. No customers.

"Ma?" I call out into the store.

It's unusually quiet in the place, and I don't just mean the lack of welcome bells. Given the fact that my ma practically called a three-alarm fire trying to get me over here, I'm not seeing any sign that she's actually in the store.

I wander past the cash register and note a couple people browsing the stacks.

"Hey, Bob." I nod at Bob Horton, who's got his reading glasses at the end of his nose. He's leaning back in a vintage—and by that, I mean old as shit—plush rocking chair, looking over some figures on a clipboard.

"Frankie." He greets me but doesn't bother looking up from his notes. Bob's always been a little off, but he owns the local electronics store. One of the last in a twenty-mile radius that's not owned by a big corporate retailer.

"Workin' or playin', Bob?" I give the old man a half smile and scan the aisles for my mother.

Bob grunts in response.

I'm used to Bob being a man of very few words, and

awkward ones when he does talk, so I give him a nod and keep on moving.

The vibe in Latterature is a cross between an elderly aunt's attic and somebody's grandma's kitchen. I can smell the familiar scents of freshly ground coffee, vintage books, and old upholstery as I walk past bookshelves and head toward the back kitchen.

Finally, the familiar scent of hair spray and perfume greets me. Evidence that Ma was here recently, along with her friends.

"Franco. Where have you been? I've been worried sick."

I turn around and look down at Lucia Bianchi. Matriarch of our family and overall force to be reckoned with.

She's short but curvy, and despite turning fifty-nine this past spring, Ma's hair is drugstore auburn, sprayed to within an inch of its life, and perfectly styled around her smiling face.

"Come here." She holds out her manicured hands, her nails perfectly colored and bedazzled with some sparkly looking things on the ends. She pulls my face close and kisses my cheek, then loops her hand through my arm and lowers her voice. "I wish you'd gotten here sooner. What took you so long? My God, son, I was about to get in the car and make sure you weren't crushed under one of those cars or something worse."

"Morbid, Ma, but thanks for the concern." I look

around us, but my mom's crew of best friends is nowhere to be found, which is unusual.

Lucia was a stay-at-home mom who never went to work even after we grew up, but by God, she made knowing the ins and outs of her kids' lives more than just her job. It was her passion.

Now that Vito, Benny, Gracie, and I are all in our thirties, Ma makes *everyone's* business her job. And unless she's with my father, she's never far from her crew of best lady friends.

"What's with the urgency? You made it sound like—"

Ma shushes me a little too vigorously and points a red nail toward the lounger where Bob is rocking back and forth. She gives me the universal mom-eyes, half wide and then settling into a frustrated glare, as she huffs, "Come back into the kitchen."

"In the kitchen? Ma, come on, I got to get back to work."

My mother ignores me and takes hold of my arm. All five foot nothing of her pedals off toward the back of the store, dragging me with her.

I would stop and argue the point, but when Lucia Bianchi gets her mind set on something, there is only one person who can stop her and that's my father, Mario.

We push through the door with an ancient, paint-chipped sign that would read *Employees Only* if all the letters were still there, but which now reads, "E p l ees On ."

As soon as we're in the back, Ma starts talking a million miles a second. "Did you see Bob out there? Franco, you've got to get rid of him." My mother's gesturing wildly, her nails like tiny daggers already dripping with Bob Horton's blood.

"Come on, Ma. What's the problem with Bob? He's harmless." As I peer around the room, the rest of Mom's crew rushes toward me, and then I get it.

The gang is all here after all.

They're all just hiding from Bob.

Carol, Jack's mom, who's currently living with him and making him sandwiches and coffee, starts first. She's wearing a low-cut fuchsia top that reveals an expanse of cleavage the likes of which I never want to see on anyone's mom.

She touches my forearm before she starts to speak. "Franco, the man's odd. You know he's odd, and his nephew's odd. The lot of those Hortons are strange. Always have been." As if she remembers that I have history with his niece, she pats my arm. "Not that sweet Celeste, though. Good thing she married and ditched the Horton last name."

I'm just about to roll my eyes and set the ladies straight, when Sassy, who's never been called by her given name of Shirley, slaps a hand against my arm. "Listen to your mother, Frankie."

Sassy waits tables at the only Italian restaurant in

town, owned by none other than my cocky, asshole younger brother Benny.

She's like a second mother to us kids, which is why she feels comfortable laying hands on me, especially in front of my own mother.

Hell, all the women in my mom's lady gang are like mothers to me. Although to be fair, Ma is more mother than any one man needs.

"Thank you, Sassy," my mother says, sounding exasperated. "You know what a pain in the ass that man is. Plus, he's..." Ma taps the tips of her long nails together while she thinks of just the right insult.

"He's got *sociopath* vibes," a voice calls from just behind Sassy.

"Bev's right." Sassy moves aside and nudges forward the quietest—which by no definition of the word means quiet—friend of my mother's. Sassy nods vigorously. "You tell him, Bev."

"Ladies, please." I hold up a hand and hold back an impatient sigh before Bev can launch into a spiel about her assessment of Bob's mental state. "You all have known Bob Horton for freakin' ever, and he's..." I have to bite back the words. "All right, he's a little off, but so what? Has he done anything? I just saw him out front, and he seemed harmless enough."

A little grumpy, but if he had the first idea that his anti-fan club was hiding out in the bookstore's café kitchen, I'd have been a grumpy asshole too.

"This isn't about us, Franco." Ma clutches the trio of

gold charms that hangs around her neck—an Italian horn, a simple cross, and an engraved heart, a gift from my father for their 25th wedding anniversary. She glares at me and steps away from her three best friends. "This is about Chloe. We can't let that lecherous creep take the girl for the little she's got. She's been through so much already."

"Chloe?" I draw in a long, calming breath and check the time on my phone. "Ma, who the hell is Chloe and what's Bob done to her?"

"Well, nothing yet, but that's why you're here." My mother, on her three-inch heels, marches through the kitchen toward the commercial refrigerator at the back of the room. "Chloe, come meet my son."

Oh, for fuck's sake.

There's another one of them.

Chloe must be the relative who has come up here to take over Latterature since Ann, the previous owner, passed.

Now it's starting to make sense.

My mom's gang just added a plus-one, and I'm being called in to rescue the old lady from what, I have no clue. But I am hoping we're getting close to the point.

"Ma, what could Bob possibly be—" But the words die in my throat.

I squint and blink, expecting my vision to clear at any moment and for a clone of Ann—short, round, and heavily age-spotted—to appear before my eyes.

But that doesn't happen.

What does happen is Sassy, Bev, Carol, and Ma form this mom-circle around me.

I can feel the weight of their meddling looks as Ma coaxes a woman who looks younger than me using a voice better suited to soothing stray puppies and lost kittens at the rescue where she volunteers with Bev.

"Chloe," Ma says, drawing out her name as though it's something precious, "this is my son Franco Bianchi. Franco, this is Chloe Harkin."

The woman in front of me is dressed the opposite of the older women huddled in the kitchen. While the lady gang is a riot of colorful tops, plunging necklines, tight jeans, and artificial nails, Chloe is...simple.

Plain, if you consider she's wearing cargo pants, combat boots, and an oversized striped sweater so big she could probably fit two of her under there and still have room. But there is nothing average about the fire in her green eyes as she looks at me, sucking a plush lower lip into her mouth.

Chloe looks away and tugs nervously on a lock of long auburn hair. "Nice to meet you," she mumbles, her voice as tiny as a mouse.

I wipe my palm on my jeans to make sure I don't have any grease left on it and hold out my hand. "I'm a mechanic," I explain. "Up at Easy Start. Welcome to Star Falls."

Chloe bites down on that lower lip and flicks a look at my mom.

"Go on," Lucia urges. "Franco doesn't bite."

I do, but that's not the kind of information a son shares with his mother.

I hold my hand firm and wait while the timid little thing sniffs, gathers her courage, and then slips her hand in mine.

Chloe gives it a quick pump, then pulls away—like she might actually believe I bite.

"You're related to Ann?" I ask, curious how this slim, pretty redhead shares blood with the lady who for years blended into my mother's friend group in every way.

This woman—or girl—God...I can't tell if she's nineteen or twenty-nine... This Chloe is nothing like Ann.

"This is Ann's niece, Franco," Sassy blurts, but after a cutting glare from my mother, Sassy presses her lips closed.

"Let Chloe talk," Lucia urges, and that's when I know.

This isn't a rescue.

This is a setup.

I inhale deeply though my nose, flaring my nostrils against the overpowering cloud of mom perfumes diluted by something lighter, cleaner. I roll my shoulders and rub my chin where a healthy growth of stubble is already fighting to break through.

I should have known.

I look from Chloe's reddening cheeks to the bright,

beaming smiles of every other woman in the room and shake my head.

"Ma," I say, drawing out my syllables so she knows I'm onto her. "It's the middle of my workday. If Bob didn't do something shady, I'm out of here."

Ma's face falls, and I know she's aware that I'm not here to play. "Franco." She sounds almost insulted. "Give me a chance to explain. You just got here. You think Jack can't handle that shop on his own for thirty minutes? Bob's sold Chloe one of those big TVs, and he's charging her—"

"I bought it. He didn't force me." Chloe's voice is soft, but if she's interrupting my mother, she has some kind of spine under that afghan-sized sweater. She gives my mother a pained but sincere smile, the honesty in it breaking something open deep in my chest. "I wanted it, Mrs. Bianchi. I've got some plans to modernize the store."

My mother waves a hand in the air dismissively. "Honey, of course, if you want it, you should buy it. But Bob Horton—"

The sound of a congested throat clearing in the doorway draws every set of eyes in the kitchen.

"Lucia, ladies." Bob Horton wipes his nose along the long sleeve of his blue work shirt, and I can feel my mother bristle beside me. "TV's up and working, Ms. Harkin. I left your copy of the installment agreement on the counter. I don't extend credit. So you miss even one payment, and I'll be back down here to take the set

13

back." He looks at Chloe harshly, and something in my gut tightens as his eyes rake over her.

I don't like the feeling.

"Your aunt was a nice lady," Bob added. "Sorry for your loss. But business is business."

The unpleasant huffing and shifting on heels from each of my mother's friends lets me know exactly how they all feel about Bob, his television, and his warning to Chloe to make the payments for the device on time.

"Thank you, Bob," Sassy says, a sneer in her voice. "You know, the girl's been through so much. You could just leave the paperwork and be done with it."

"It's just business," he repeats in a sort of insulted pout, sniffling loud enough that I almost instinctively look around for a tissue.

Instead, I nod at Chloe. "You good? You wanted this TV?"

Her lower lip is between her teeth when she nods and finally releases it. "Yes, I do. Thank you, Mr. Horton."

She'll learn soon enough that nobody under the age of seventy goes by a title around here. Instead, I nod at Bob and clap him on the shoulder. "I'll walk you out."

I follow the man to the front and notice that in the time it takes me to walk back through the store, Bob's nephew, Tyler, has pulled up and is idling their shitty company pickup beside my bike.

"Hey, Ty." I lift my chin at the kid. "How's the starter? Any better?"

Tyler nods. "Yeah," he grumbles, avoiding eye contact. "Been running fine," he adds, his voice weirdly close to a whisper.

I watch as Bob climbs into the passenger seat, mumbles something to his nephew, and they take off.

When I turn back to Latterature, four old ladies are watching me through the glass. I yank open the door, and I swim through the sea of colorful blouses. "See that?" I ask, gesturing toward the door. "Bob's gone. You can all go on and pick on some other aging electronics salesman."

Bev and Sassy start talking between themselves, while Carol tugs my mom's arm and points to the large television that Bob set up in the reading nook.

It seems like my work here is done, but I feel Chloe's eyes on me. I turn to her and watch as a pretty shade of pink brightens her cheeks.

I don't know if this woman was in on my mother summoning me over here, but even if she was, she's only in town because she suffered a loss.

"I'm sorry about your aunt," I say sincerely, meaning every word. "She was a great lady. Made my favorite sandwich in all of Star Falls."

Chloe's whole body seems to relax at the mention of her aunt. "Mine too," she says. "Grilled cheese with chicken and bacon. She made it special every time she visited my mom and me."

I cover my belly with both hands and groan in spite of myself. "That's the one. My favorite sandwich. Just don't tell my brother I said that. He's a cocky son of a bitch when it comes to food."

"Franco, maybe you should take Chloe to dinner tonight." Ma has disentangled herself from Carol and has nosed her way between me and the new owner of Latterature. "She's new to town and doesn't know anyone. Take her to your brother's restaurant. You do like Italian food, don't you, dear?"

"Oh no, that's… I mean… Yes, I like Italian, but…" Chloe's stammering, but her eyes are searching my face. An innocent, sweet smile brings light to those green eyes. "You don't have to. I…I'm fine, really. I have so much to do here in the store."

I'm looking her over, the long, luscious locks of auburn hair and that sweet face that somehow doesn't match the dowdy, nerdy clothes she's wearing.

I see just a hint of the curves buried beneath the blanket-like layers, and my fingers suddenly itch to peel them back one by one.

And then I stop myself.

Something about the woman has my body paying attention.

My gut tightens at the way she's biting her bottom lip again, and I wonder if she likes being bitten as much as she seems to like biting.

But my mother's voice is in my ears, loudly demanding that I take Chloe on a date, and I know right there I have to put a stop to the whole thing. If I let myself get set up by my mother once, my entire life will become an episode of *Matchmaking with Lucia and Company*.

"Chloe, no offense, but this—" I motion toward Ma and her lady gang "—is my mother's not-at-all subtle attempt to set her single son up with the new—and I assume single—woman in town." I give Ma a sharp glare.

"She is single," Ma adds. "That was the first thing I asked, son. I'm not trying to wreck a happy home here."

I nod. "Hmm-mm," I mutter. "Thought so." I lean down and plant a kiss on my mother's hair, and she swats me away before fluffing the curls that I flattened back into place. "Ma, I'll talk to you later. Chloe, it was nice meeting you. Enjoy the television." I point at Bev, Sassy, and Carol, all of whom are standing by just waiting, like they'll break out into applause if I agree to take Chloe to dinner. "Ladies." I nod. "I'd appreciate if the next time my ma gets an idea in her head related to my love life, you'll remind her—" I grab the door handle and yank it open "—to butt out."

I hear a chorus of disappointed sighs as one by one the ladies say goodbye.

"We only want what's best for you, Franco."

"Your mother means well, Frankie."

"I told you this wasn't going to work, Lucia. Your son isn't the dating kind."

Isn't the dating kind?

That stops me in my tracks, but if I go back in, I'm only inviting the lot of them to start analyzing my love

17

life. And I've had more than enough time on that topic for one day.

I almost turn back to defend myself, but a frustrated grunt comes out instead, and I decide it's better to leave all this before I start something I really don't want to finish. I tug my sunglasses over my eyes, then climb onto my bike and toss a glare back toward the store since I know every one of them is still standing at the door, watching me pull away.

And curiously enough, so is Chloe.

CHAPTER 2
CHLOE

I WATCH the most gorgeous man I've ever seen kick a thick leg over his bike and ride off into the sunset.

I realize the entire crowd of women is chattering and arguing with one another, while I'm standing here gaping after Lucia's son like a starving puppy.

It's been ages since I had a date, and I don't think any of the guys I've been out with since I broke it off with David compare to the heavily tattooed, muscular man I just met. Not in the looks department—or in the attitude either.

Franco Bianchi.

My skin pebbles just thinking his name, and I nervously bite on my lower lip. There are words for guys like Franco: sexy, powerful, and totally out of my league.

Much as I'm sure Lucia would have been thrilled if her son had taken me out, it would have been nothing more than a pity date. An awkward dinner to appease his mother, and nothing at all to do with me.

I'm as forgettable as yesterday's lunch to a guy like that, and much as Lucia might have good intentions, even thinking about it hurts a little.

I wonder if my thoughts are showing all over my face because Lucia looks like she feels terrible.

"Chloe, I feel like I have to apologize for my son." She's standing in front of me, clutching her necklace. Her face is tight, her lips pressed thin. "Franco is such a good boy. He's not normally so rude and so…"

"Do you blame him, Lucia?" The one called Sassy has a hand on her hip and one perfectly drawn-on eyebrow cocked almost to her hairline. "Franco's a grown man. He doesn't want his mother meddling in his love life."

"Whose side are you on, Sas?" Bev hisses.

My aunt had a very special relationship with Bev, the lady who runs the local animal shelter.

I am only just learning how many amazing relationships my aunt Ann had here in Star Falls. I can now understand why she spent so many years here, running this small bookstore and café, despite the fact that she was losing money hand over fist.

"Why do you need this expensive TV, anyway?"

The sudden silence in the store lets me know I drifted off into my own thoughts again. "I'm sorry." I blink and look from Lucia to Bev, then from Sassy to

Carol, before flushing so hard I can feel my cheeks go pink. "I missed the question?"

The ladies all start talking over one another about the television and Franco, but I notice a customer standing near the front door, looking like the crew of women is blocking her way in. I tug open the glass door, and a gorgeous woman with long, glossy black hair and sunglasses over her eyes clomps into the store.

"Ma. What the eff?" She tears the sunglasses away from her face and stares at each woman in turn.

I have no idea which one is her mother, but once I see her eyes, I have a pretty good guess.

She points a heavily tattooed hand at Lucia. "Where you been with the car all morning? You were supposed to drive me to work."

Lucia gasps and looks horrified. "I'm sorry, Gracie. I met the girls down here for an emergency."

"I had to wake up Vito for a ride. Dad drove out to Cleveland just after you left."

"Why on earth did he go to Cleveland without me?" Lucia starts fumbling for her phone, which is encased in a glittery pink protective sleeve. "That man shouldn't be driving until he gets a pair of real glasses. I don't know how he's going to see the signs on the highway."

Gracie grabs the device from her mom and flips a little button. "See, Ma? Your phone was on silent. The entire family could have been calling for help, and you wouldn't have known. Dad must've called five times before he left."

Lucia shakes her head and holds the phone in her hands like it's an explosive device and Grace is the detonation expert who just neutralized the threat. "Oh, son of a gun. I was wondering why I wasn't getting any calls after I texted your brother."

Grace lifts a brow and strikes a dramatic pose.

I'm captivated by her larger-than-life attitude and colorful tattoos.

She jams the sunglasses on top of her head and softens as she looks at each of her mother's friends. "Bev, Sassy, Carol." She kisses each woman on the cheek before turning back to her mother. "Mom, what the hell kind of emergency could you have at a bookstore?"

I squirm a little bit, feeling like I'm drowning in my striped sweater. Next to Grace, who's wearing a shredded concert T-shirt with more holes than fabric, I feel every bit the bookish nerd that I am.

I start to tiptoe backward, hoping to slip unnoticed into the kitchen.

Sassy points a finger at me before I can get away. "That," she says, narrowing her thickly mascaraed eyes at me. "That's the emergency."

Grace looks me over, and it feels like I'm in fifth grade again. I nearly lean against the wall for support under the confident, bold woman's gaze.

Grace squints a little and cocks her head. "Who's this?" she asks, not even addressing her question to me.

Yeah, if I felt invisible before, I feel like a piece of

furniture now. "I'm—" I wring my hands together, then awkwardly stick one out toward Grace.

Lucia cuts me off before I can finish introducing myself. "Gracie. This is Ann's niece. I've been talking about her all week, for goodness' sake." Lucia puts a hand on my arm, a thin stack of gold bangle bracelets clicking wildly with the movement. "This is Chloe Harkin."

Grace twists her lips to one side, and a deep dimple marks her cheek. Grace is the kind of girl everyone wanted to be in high school. Cool, pretty, and completely indifferent to what anyone else thinks.

I can already see the family resemblance to her older brother. My heart thumps an excited beat in my chest as I picture Franco's thick waves of hair and piercing eyes. His, though, were blue.

She eyes me curiously, silent for a moment, and then slaps the shredded knee of her black jeans and curses. "I got it now." Instead of shaking my awkwardly outstretched hand, Grace turns to her mom. "This is the girl you were trying to set Frankie up with?"

"Look at her." Lucia crows. "She's a doll. Your brother could use a nice girl like Chloe. Before all the other dogs in this town come sniffing around wanting a shot at the new girl."

I surprise myself by snorting at that. No dogs have ever come sniffing around me. I'm sure Star Falls won't be any different. Not if the women look like Grace, and the men... Well, if the men look like Franco, I may as well put on a habit and turn this bookstore into a convent. I've got as much chance with a guy like that as a nun does.

Sassy puts an end to the conversation by swinging her oversized metallic silver purse over her shoulder. "Gals, I got to run. My boss is a real asshole if I'm late, and I've got to stop home for my uniform."

"Asshole boss." Lucia scowls, but it's clear she's not insulted. "You tell that son of mine to call his mother. Benito hasn't called in days."

"He's sleeping with that new bartender he hired," Grace says with a smirk.

Sassy grumbles. "This week, he is. And last week, it was another one, and next week, it'll be someone else."

Lucia shakes her head, sighing as if the weight of the world rests on her tiny shoulders. "Is it too much to ask that my children settle down and be happy? What is it with all this sexual freedom? When I was young…"

There's a groan from one of the women.

"And that's my cue to go." Sassy air-kisses her friends goodbye and waves at me before breezing out of the store.

Lucia continues, undeterred. "And would it be so much to ask for grandchildren while I'm still healthy enough to enjoy them?" She looks at me, a sadness in her face. "Tomorrow isn't promised to anyone, and I just want grandbabies I can push in their strollers. I don't want them pushing me in mine."

"So, you're Ann's niece?" Grace asks, completely

ignoring her mother's pity party as she finally holds out her hand to me.

I nod. "I'm Chloe Harkin. Nice to meet you."

Grace seems to size me up as she takes in my sweater and cargo boots. She releases my hand with a nod. "I work next door at The Body Shop. You'll be seeing a lot of me, as long as you keep making that kick-ass coffee your aunt used to make. I'm literally addicted to her peanut butter crisps too. I'm Gracie, and that one belongs to me." She lifts one of those perfect brows impossibly higher and jerks a thumb toward Lucia.

Of course Gracie works at the town tattoo parlor. If she got any cooler, I might just collapse into a heap of dust on the floor.

"Just so you know," she says, gesturing toward her mother. "My ma's going to try to set you up with her oldest son until you tell her in no uncertain terms to lay the fuck off the matchmaking. Either you tell her, or my brother will."

"I didn't teach my daughter to cuss like a sailor," Lucia says, sounding a little hurt. "And what's so wrong with wanting to see my children happy?"

"Ma, what do you even know about this girl?" Gracie demands. She waves a hand at me. "Look at her. She might not even be into guys, for all you know. You can't just go around trying to hook up your kids with anything that lives and breathes and hasn't yet slept with Benito." She whips her head, and her long black locks

27

go flying. "You haven't, have you? My brother does get around pretty damn quick."

Lucia makes the sign of the cross over her chest and forehead. "The girl's been here two weeks. Not even your brother moves that fast."

"Yes, he does," they say, and by they, I mean all of them—Bev, Carol, and Gracie.

Lucia purses her lips, reluctantly admitting they are right. "Fine. Maybe I should have asked whether Chloe is attracted to men and whether she's already had relations with my youngest son before I tried to set her up with Franco. I'm just trying to help here."

"Help by not helping," Grace says, then she points a finger at me. "You got any coffee? I'd kill for a shot of caffeine and a peanut butter crisp."

I nod, remembering that I do actually have a business to run, and this place is not just a social club for my aunt's friends. "I'll start a fresh pot," I tell her. "Give me about five minutes."

Grace drops her sunglasses back over her eyes and clomps toward the door. "I'll stop back," she says over her shoulder. "I got to open next door."

I scurry back toward the kitchen, wishing for the millionth time since I set foot in Latterature that my aunt had a peekaboo window in the kitchen.

Before I push past the kitchen door, I hear Lucia call my name. "Chloe, sweetheart. We're leaving."

I hustle back to the front to wish the women good-bye. They hardly seem to notice me. Bev and Lucia are talking about covering shifts at the local animal shelter. Carol is adjusting the top of her blouse, asking if it sends the wrong message for a first date.

"It's coffee with Ray Morris, Carol. What kind of messages do you think that man is going to pick up on from a blouse?" Bev is unzipping a fanny pack that is hanging around her waist and then digging around for her car keys. "Besides," she adds, a heavy note of judgment in her tone. "Aren't you and Earl still married?"

Carol primly adjusts the fuchsia top to cover her cleavage with a bit more modesty. "We're separated," she clarifies. "And it's complicated. These things take time. While Earl is sorting out what he needs, well…in the meantime, I'm sorting out mine."

Bev barks a rough laugh. "For the love of all that's holy, Carol, don't let Ray Morris be the one to scratch your feminine itch. And if he does, please don't tell us about it."

They are all giggling and talking, but as Lucia pulls open the door and holds it for her friends, she cocks her chin and calls out to me. "Chloe, honey. Where're your aunt's welcome bells? You don't want to be in the back and not know if a customer comes in the store!"

I nod and scan the floor and the front counter, but I don't see them. "Bob's nephew took them down when they came to deliver the television." He'd said the constant ringing would be noise we didn't need while they were going in and out. But it looks like he didn't replace them before they left. "I'll find them," I assure her. "Thanks."

She is fussing with a pair of massive sunglasses when she shouts to her friends and trots back into the shop.

"Chloe, you should come to my place for dinner on Sunday." She's breathless and looks excited, like she's just been hit with inspiration. "My husband cooks, and Mario…" She pinches her thumb and fingers together, the tips of her nails clicking lightly, then kisses them and gestures at me with her hand in something that looks like delight. "He's the real cook in the family. Home-cooked Italian food and good company. The whole family will be there…including my Franco." She leans in a little closer and says in a hushed voice, "And don't even think about bringing anything. You're not a guest. You're family."

I give her a weak smile. The thought of sitting down to eat with the bold, outrageous Bianchi family is a lot to take in.

"I'll try to make it," I say vaguely. "I have so much work to do here in the shop."

"It's dinner. You got to eat, and you haven't eaten until you've had my husband's meatballs. You can't say no to Mario's meatballs. Oh, maybe I can get him to make braciole. It's to die for. He'll do it. He'll make it just for you. I'll see you at six sharp, honey."

She doesn't wait for me to respond and hustles down the block toward her ridiculously huge pickup truck. I

30

can see just the top of her auburn-colored hair as she steps up on the running board and climbs behind the steering wheel of the burgundy beast.

I head back inside Latterature. As overwhelmed as I was by the noise and color and chaos of Aunt Ann's friends, somehow, without them here, everything in the shop seems strangely quiet and extremely lonely.

CHAPTER 3
FRANCO

I ROLL INTO MY PARENTS' house close to an hour before dinner is served because I know if I'm not there to set the table, Vito will do it and he'll fuck it all up.

Of the four of us Bianchi siblings, two still live at home. Gracie, because even though she's thirty, she's the baby, and Ma and Pops give her absolutely no reason to move from the comforts of her childhood home.

And then there's Vito.

We're eleven months apart and practically went through everything at the same time, and yet we turned out to be two totally different men.

We both like to work with our hands, but that's where the similarities end. Vito's a firefighter, and, to him, mealtime means setting out a stack of plates, a jumble of mismatched silverware, and letting everybody help themselves.

Ma likes things a certain way, and while it may be extra work to pull out the cloth napkins and put the leaf in the dining room table, it makes her happy.

Over the years, we've each fallen into roles in the family.

Gracie is the baby, so she's off the hook, no matter what the issue is. I'm surprised Ma and Pops even make her clear her own plate. She's spoiled fucking rotten and can do no wrong.

Benito, the second youngest, owns an Italian restaurant, but does he lift a finger to help Pops make dinner? Hell no. He can hardly pull himself from his restaurant most weekends for the couple hours it takes to eat and socialize before bolting out the door like he's a CEO and not a chef.

Benny's cocky, annoying, arrogant, and hilarious, but what makes it so frustrating is he's a genuinely good guy. He's got the quickest temper of all of us, but he's driven, generous, and a lot of other good qualities that I'll never admit to his face. He's a brilliant cook, having picked up a ton over the years from our parents and grandparents. But when he comes home, he's all youngest son. The brilliant cook and demanding chef in him take a back seat, and he just lets himself be served and babied. Cocksucker.

And then there's me. The oldest. The one who moved out first—much to my parents' horror—and who is probably the most responsible. I pay attention to my parents and what they need, even if they drive me up a fucking wall sometimes.

They're family.

Wherever they are is my forever home, so even though I don't live under their roof anymore, I show up early enough for table-setting duty.

But today when I arrive, the table's already set. And not only that, the table's set for seven.

There's never an extra place setting.

"Why's it so quiet in here?" I hang my keys on the wall cabinet by the front door Pops built Ma after he retired. I nod at the dining room table, which I can see from the entryway. I kick off my boots and lift my brows at Gracie, who is snuggled down on the leather sectional nibbling the ends of her hair while she watches a football game.

Gracie doesn't bother looking up. "Franco," she mumbles in greeting, her eyes locked on the huge screen that hangs over the fireplace.

I drop down onto the couch, annoyingly close to Gracie. A huge, warm lump tucked under a crocheted afghan shifts as I rest my head on my sister's shoulder. "Ladies," I say, greeting my mother's dogs. "Soooo." I bat my eyelashes dramatically. "Watching your man play today?"

"Shut up, heathen." Grace reaches past the dogs to shove me away, but I grab her wrists and hold them tight, locked in an eternal brother-sister wrestling match.

35

"Come on, Gracie. You can admit you've got a crush on that boy." I release her hands when Venus, the most vicious of my mother's dogs, starts barking. I stand beside the armrest and lean down to kiss the top of Grace's hair. "Serious now. Are you all right?" I ask.

Gracie looks up at me, a moment's softness overtaking her hard glare. "Let it go, all right?" The vulnerability and sorrow in her eyes almost crack my heart in two.

My sister doesn't normally look sad. Her happiness is infectious, and her rage is entertaining. I don't like this other place she's been in lately. This melancholy, withdrawn space. But since she's flipped the switch, I'm not about to drag her back down into something she clearly doesn't want to talk about.

Before I ask anything, she sets her lips in a line and jabs a finger into my chest. "Go change your socks. You stink, and Ma invited some girl over for dinner."

I know for a fact that my feet don't stink, but I lift my leg as far as I can and wiggle my toes at her. "You want to eat my sock? Keep it up."

I drop the jokes and rest my ass on the armrest before Ma sees me and yells at me that I'm going to break the sofa. I stare daggers at the television where the most recent guy who broke my sister's heart is playing defense for the Browns.

This past spring, my sister tattooed a customer, and after she finished, they ended up having some hot and heavy fling.

Turns out he's a major player and not just on the ball field. Gracie's a good girl. Smart, gorgeous. But she's got awful taste in men.

"We could watch the news if you just want to fall into a pit of depression," I remind her, trying to lighten the mood. I tug on the ends of her hair but can't even coax a smile out of her.

She flicks my hand away. "Worry about yourself, Romeo," she says. "Ma's got a bug up her butt to marry you off."

I sigh and quickly yank myself off the arm of the couch as I hear Ma's voice on the phone echoing through the house. "This is going to be some dinner," I mutter and head over to the table to inspect the settings.

Ma must have set it herself, because not only is the fall harvest tablecloth with matching napkins and bronze-colored maple leaf napkin rings already set for seven, I notice little pieces of paper with everyone's name written out on them in my mom's perfect cursive handwriting. I'm not even surprised when I see I've been assigned a seat next to Chloe.

My breath catches a little in my chest as I think about Ann's niece. It's a weird reaction—part resistance and maybe part something else. But I'm not sure what, and I sure as hell don't want to think about that right now.

"What's the bookstore girl doing at family dinner?" I bark out at no one in particular.

Ma shifts immediately from whatever conversation

she's having on her cell phone to answering me. "Shh, Franco. I'm on the phone. Go open the wine. It needs to breathe."

I shake my head and wander into the kitchen.

My father is standing at the small butcher block island, a well-worn red apron protecting his navy flannel shirt from splatters. He's got a pair of reading glasses perched on the end of his nose, and he's glaring at a package of breadsticks.

"Son, what does this say?" Without even a hello, Pops shoves the glasses onto the mountain of wavy silver hair that almost perfectly matches mine in thickness and style and scowls. He scrubs a hand over the white bristles on his chin. "It might be time for something stronger than drugstore cheaters."

I take the package from him, then lean in and kiss him on the cheek, taking in his familiar cologne that's fighting for dominance over the massive pot of sauce that's bubbling on the stove.

"Gluten-free rosemary garlic grissini," I tell him, reading the label. "You cutting back on gluten, Pops?"

He lifts his hands in surrender. "So, I grabbed the wrong package. There's going to be enough gluten at the table to smother a hippo. A gluten-free breadstick ain't going to kill anybody." He motions to me with an aged, muscular hand. "Open that, and put them in a basket before your mother sees the package."

I tear open the extremely loud plastic wrapper and sniff the contents. "Mmm." I take one of the grissini and give it a bite. "I don't care what these are or are not made of. They taste damn good," I assure him. "You get these at the specialty market the other day?" I smack my lips and dig in a cabinet for the woven cloth basket Ma likes to serve bread in.

My dad nods. "Probably the last time I'll drive that far until I get my eyes looked at. Don't get old, son. Aging's a bitch, and not the good kind."

"So, go to the eye doctor," I tell him. "It'll get Ma off your back, and then you can drive all over the state looking for cooking stores. It's a pair of glasses. What's the big deal?"

Dad's bent over the stove stirring one pot, checking the contents of the oven, and clicking off the kitchen timer just as it dings. "Yeah, yeah," he says. "I'll go, I'll go. I've been busy. Open the wine, Franco. Two bottles tonight. Your mother invited a guest."

I rummage in the junk drawer for the bottle opener. "About that," I grumble, turning to face my pops. "Why the hell is Ma inviting somebody to dinner?"

My father echoes his favorite catchphrase as he turns to check on the braciole. "What's the big deal? It's one more person."

I can't tell if my father is in on Mom's plans to hook me up with her definition of a "sweet girl," or if he's choosing when and how exactly to battle his wife. An invitation to dinner is one thing. I can grin and be civil, but what Ma doesn't know is a meal with the Bianchis is probably the worst way to entice Chloe to go out with me.

One evening with all of us at the table and the woman will go running back to wherever it is she came from before she moved to Star Falls.

I'm in the dining room uncorking our family's favorite wine when Vito comes tumbling up the basement stairs, a pair of flowery oven mitts on his hands.

"Hey, asshole." I nod at him. "What's for dessert?"

One of the reasons my parents bought this house just after Gracie was born was the second kitchen in the basement.

"What's it smell like, dicknose?" Vito rushes past me, headed for the kitchen.

I shake my head. He never learns. I uncork the second bottle of cab and wait for my dad to yell.

"Vito, where do you think I'm going to find room for the cake to cool up here? Take it back downstairs, and put it on the cooling rack like I told you." My father isn't really mad. More like impatient.

Vito, like I said, ain't nothing like me. He doesn't always think and mostly just runs around like a clueless, curious puppy.

After more than thirty-five years as Mario Bianchi's son, you'd think he'd know not to bring dessert upstairs until some space has been cleared after the meal.

"Shit, yeah. Yeah. Sorry, Pops." Vito comes shuffling back, his bare feet in a pair of open-toe house slippers dragging along the tile floors and a pair of threadbare flannel PJ bottoms sagging at his waist.

"You going to dress for dinner?" I call after him. "Ma invited a guest."

He throws a scowl over his shoulder at me. "A guest? What the fuck?"

"Language, Vito." My mother is still on the phone but manages to hear my brother curse from someplace deep inside the house.

I stifle a grin and set the bottles of wine on the table to breathe. I'm about to head back to the kitchen to help Dad when there's a soft movement against my ankles.

"V!" I shout, bending down to pick up another of Ma's rescues. "One of the cats got out of the basement."

I pick the thing up, and it immediately melts into a vibrating engine of purring as I rub behind its ears. I stalk down the basement stairs, pulling the door closed behind me. "Dumbass, you know to keep the cats locked up down here while Dad's cooking." I set the cat down gently on the cool tile floor of the basement.

Vito is setting the pineapple upside-down cake on the cooling rack on the basement kitchen counter—which he should have done in the first place. "Yeah, yeah, it's fine," he grumbles.

He covers the cake with parchment paper and then grabs a cat toy that looks like a feather at the end of a fishing pole and coaxes the cat back into my old bedroom.

I pull back the paper and sniff the cake. The buttery

brown sugar topping is perfectly glazed, locking the bright red maraschino cherries right in the centers of the canned pineapple rings.

It ain't fancy, but it's a taste of home. Of tradition. Of family.

"Go change," I tell him. "You're going to give our mother a heart attack in that getup."

"It's my day off. Just want to be fucking comfy." Vito stomps up the stairs, and I hear him slam the basement door before he clomps through the house.

"Franco!" My mother's shouts echo through the basement.

I check the door to my old bedroom to make sure Fred and Ginger are secure, but Ma's already halfway down the stairs. "Honey, no. Let the cats out." Ma is a blur of tight denim, red hair, and jangling bracelets as she rushes past me.

"Why? I thought you wanted them locked up when Dad's cooking?" I cock my chin and watch as Ma carries one cat and then the other out from my old room.

"I'm fostering a doggie mama, Franco, and the cats make her nervous." Ma checks the water and food dishes and strokes the head of the dog who clearly trusts her. "She's going to be a hard one to give up," my mom says thoughtfully. She does a quick check of each puppy, six in all, and then stands. "She is very gentle but already very protective of me and your father. Isn't she gorgeous, honey? Don't you think you might want a puppy when they're old enough? You live all by your-self in that house…"

"Ma." I shake my head. "You know I'm renting, and I'm not home enough to take care of a puppy." I watch the way the dog tracks my mother's every move, as if she'd haul herself from a nest of puppies to protect Ma if I made the slightest wrong move. "What are they?" I ask.

My mother shrugs. "Hard to say. She came into the shelter pregnant. Time will tell." She loops her arm through mine, and we head upstairs. "Think about it. A puppy would be good for you."

Before I can remind her again why that would *not* be good for me, the doorbell rings.

"Oh, that must be Chloe." Ma hustles the rest of the way upstairs, and I follow, closing the basement door behind me. Dolce and Venus both start barking, and Ma turns her attention to the dogs. "Franco, you get the door."

While Gracie holds Venus in her arms and shushes her, Ma makes sure Dolce gets off the couch without hurting her aging hips.

I have no clue what my mother told Chloe to entice the woman to come for family dinner, so I sigh and brace myself for the inevitable awkwardness.

When I open the door, the only thing that's awkward is the little catch in my throat.

The sun is setting, and somehow the light catches on Chloe's green eyes in a way that takes my breath away.

She looks lost for a moment, shocked or maybe confused that I opened the door and not my mother.

I stare at her without greeting her, licking my lips on instinct as I study her eyes, her hair, the sweet curve of her lips.

She smiles apologetically, ducking her head a little as if she's embarrassed to be here. "Hi, Franco. I'm Chloe. We met the other day at my aunt's café." She says it like a question, as though she doesn't expect me to remember her.

She's standing there holding a plate covered with foil and a small bouquet of flowers. She's wearing something slightly less gigantic than the other day.

"Franco. Let her in." Mom's cry from the living room nudges me into movement.

"Yeah," I say, shaking my head and scowling at the blood that surges through my limbs. I'm thirty-eight, not eighteen. Why the hell does this woman in bag-lady clothes make me feel like a kid? "I remember you," I say gruffly, covering my confusion. "Come in."

She steps past me and stops, her eyes on the floor. "Umm," she mumbles, thrusting the plate in my direction. "Would you mind holding this while I take off my boots?"

I take the plate from her and the flowers. I assume she needs both hands to take off those boots, so I just stand there, like a kid who's never seen a woman's behind before, watching her bend over to unlace the boots.

She leans a hip against the wall to balance herself while she slides her feet from the boots, then she smooths her hair and adjusts the sweater so that, if it were actually possible, it covers even more of her. She tugs it past her waist so it covers the fine curve of her ass, and then she slips her hands deep inside the sleeves.

"I brought my aunt's peanut butter crisp cookies. I hope that's okay?" She's looking at me, studying my chin like there's something stuck there, and very definitely avoiding my eyes.

I self-consciously swipe at my chin with my forearm just in case I have dog hair or something there since I've got her plate of cookies in one hand and the flowers in the other. "Yeah," I say distractedly, "great."

Being reduced to a babbling idiot by a woman's halfway-decent backside sends me into an even fouler mood.

I don't know what it is about Chloe that's turned me stone stupid, but I'm annoyed with myself. I'm even more annoyed with my mother for bringing a non-family member into our dinner, with my brothers for being idiots, and, if I'm reaching, with my sister just because she's been so down and won't let anyone in.

I just want to get through this dinner and get the fuck out of here.

My mother comes to the door to greet Chloe with as much enthusiasm as a one-woman parade. She's cooing and rushing up to us, all excitement and warmth.

Gracie is holding Venus in her arms, and Dolce

slowly plods behind them, her tail slapping the wall as she walks carefully down the hallway on her old dog hips.

"Chloe." Lucia opens her arms and gives me a look. "I told you not to bring anything. You're family."

I can't help rolling my eyes because, no, this woman is not family. But I instantly feel shitty for the impulse.

Chloe has done nothing wrong. Despite the fact that my mother seems hell-bent on fixing me up with any eligible female in Star Falls, I do have two brothers. Vito and Benny aren't half bad. Maybe she'll fall for one of them and I'll be off the hook.

"Did I hear someone say peanut butter crisps?" Gracie holds her body at an awkward angle, keeping snarling little Venus as far away as she can while giving Chloe a one-armed hug. "You're my new favorite person."

"Who is this?" Chloe asks, her voice a nearly breathless whisper. The honey in her voice sends a little pulse from my gut straight to my cock.

I shake my head to clear that shit away. She's whispering at a snarling Chihuahua, but my body is acting like that sweet, low rasp is meant just for me.

"Here," I grunt, thrusting the plate of cookies at my sister.

She raises a sharply angled eyebrow at me but takes the plate. I hear Chloe and Gracie cooing over the dogs, because now, of course, Dulce is sniffing and wagging all over Chloe's legs while Mom's overly loud voice booms introductions to the dogs.

Christ.

Normally, I wouldn't even notice that Ma's rolling out the red carpet for a guest, but something about the whole situation grates on me.

It's as if everyone in the family is conspiring to welcome this girl, and I'm the asshole who just wants a family dinner without the pressure of making small talk with a stranger.

A stranger who my mother seems determined to see me dating, while my body is being a traitor with the way it's reacting to her presence.

I stalk into the dining room in search of a vase for the flowers, but then I think better of it and head toward the kitchen. Dad and some cold water—for the flowers, not for me—will clear me of the shit mood I'm in now.

"Flowers?" Dad asks, pointing to a cabinet.

I grunt. "I know where the vases are." The words come out saltier than I intend, and Mario takes notice.

"What's the matter with you?" he asks. He's yanking off the apron with one hand and turning off the burners with the other. "You look like you spilled your last beer."

I yank open a cabinet and pull out a vase, then jam the small bouquet inside. "Nothing, I'm fine. When do we eat?"

Mario looks me over but doesn't push. "Benito here yet?"

47

I shake my head. "Course not."

"Your brother is a…" Dad uses a pair of tongs to extract a single strand of pasta from a stockpot of boiling water. He can tell by the way it bends how much longer it needs to cook. "Send him a text, will you? Pasta's on in three minutes, and his ass better be in his chair at the table."

I fill the vase with water and set the thing down in Dad's huge sunny window box over the sink, next to cut herbs in water-filled mason jars.

"Put those on the table," my pops urges, giving me an eyebrow raise that rivals Gracie's. "What's gotten into you in the last five minutes? Is it that girl your mother invited over?"

I take the vase back and scold myself for being so transparent. And for being such a dick. "Nah, I'm fine. Just hungry, and I'm sick of Benny always being late."

"He owns a business," my dad says with a wave of his hand. "But if I'm being honest, it bothers me too. Your brother can be a real pain in the ass."

I'm not sure if my dad's trying to make a joke so I lighten up or if he's serious. Either way, I clap him on the back and head back to the dining room.

While I set the flowers on the table, I tell myself to calm the fuck down. Just because Ma wants to set me up…it doesn't mean anything.

She's tried a million times before, although this is the first time she's ever taken her meddling match-making this far.

It's one meal.

I'll be pleasant to Chloe, ignore my mother's heavy-handed hints, eat a delicious meal, and head the fuck out.

In fact, maybe I'll even crash Benito's restaurant tonight and have a cocktail with my brother. He's a dick, but he gives me at least two rounds on the house any time I stop in.

Tonight would be a good night for a gin and tonic and some mindless conversation with the new bartender my brother's banging.

At least no one will be trying to set her up with me.

By the time I get the flowers put down, Chloe and Gracie are settled on the couch, and to my absolute shock, Venus is curled up on Chloe's lap. She looks like she might pounce at any time, but this is the only time I've seen the old dog warm up to anyone who isn't Ma or Grace.

Vito tumbles down the stairs, his wet hair flapping in his face, and interrupts their chatter. Ma introduces him to Chloe, and they all exclaim in a new round of admiration that Chloe has tamed the snarky Venus.

I watch Chloe's face, all shy smiles and self-conscious flushes, as they talk about her like she's not standing right there, and something curls around my heart.

I hate the sensation, something all fluttery and unsettled sinking deep into my chest.

I am actually relieved when I hear the front door open, and my brother Benito starts bellowing.

"I'm here!" Benny shouts and slams the door behind him before kicking off his shoes.

"You were almost late!" my mother shouts back from the living room. "Your father got ten more gray hairs waiting."

"Bullshit." Benito strides into the living room, looks over the group, and leans down to kiss my mother. Noticing Chloe, he adds, "Pardon my language. I didn't realize we had a guest."

Benny kisses our sister and slaps Vito on the back, then extends a hand to Chloe. I can see his body language change immediately, and he straightens his shoulders and lifts his chin.

"I'm Benito," he says. "And you are?"

She takes his hand much more quickly than she took mine the other day, and I have to fight a prickle of white-hot jealousy. Which is absolutely stupid, not to mention unreasonable.

First of all, my brother is a player. He's like this with every woman he meets.

Second, not five minutes ago, I was hoping Chloe *would* show an interest in one of my brothers and take the pressure off me. I should just sit back and enjoy the show.

But now, with Venus in Chloe's arms, Ma batting her eyelashes, and Benny and Vito turning on the charm, I'm not sure what I feel.

Pops comes into the living room and jerks a thumb at me. "Everything's ready," he says, which is my cue to start bringing the food to the table.

We eat family style, so every serving platter and bowl in the house needs to be filled and set out.

"Son," he says to Benny, giving my brother a smooch on the cheek. "One of these times, you could try to come more than ten seconds before we sit." Pops slows, and his voice softens as he approaches Chloe. "And you must be Chloe. Nice to finally meet you, sweetheart. You're all I've heard about for weeks now."

Chloe stands with Venus in her arms and says something I can't fully make out. But I must be staring at her, because as soon as Pops kisses her cheek and adds his surprise to everyone else's that Chloe's managed to tame the beast in Venus, my dad turns to me.

"You okay, son?" He squints at me but then motions with a thumb to my brothers. "One of you help Franco bring out the food."

"I got it," I grunt, realizing I'm the only one who seems pissed off and sour.

Even Gracie seems to warm to Chloe and is more animated and friendly than she is at a normal dinner.

"Franco." I hear disappointment in my mother's voice.

"What is it?" I pause on my way to the kitchen. "I need to help Pops serve."

Ma is glaring at the table where I've rearranged the

place settings. She shakes her head but doesn't argue with me.

I pound my way into the kitchen and take a deep breath.

It's one dinner.

Then it'll be over, and I can tell Ma to stop trying to set me up for good.

CHAPTER 4
CHLOE

FAMILY DINNER with the Bianchis is...*a lot.*

"So, Chloe..." Lucia is filling my plate with food.

I shift nervously in my seat and fiddle with the buttons on my sweater.

She loads me up with some rolled thing that looks like meat drenched in sauce, forks a pile of noodles so high I'd need a week to eat my way through it, and then uses wooden salad tongs to fill a bowl beside my plate with greens. "How do you take your pasta? Swimming in sauce or lightly coated?"

"Whatever way you want to make it," I tell her.

Mario is pouring me a very full glass of wine. "Do you drink, sweetheart? I should've asked before I started pouring."

"She'll drink if she wants it," Lucia says as she hands me a giant plate of pasta.

I just nod and murmur, "Thank you."

Grace holds up her empty glass for her father to fill more than the half glass he's already poured. "Top it off, Dad. You opened two bottles."

He fills it, and once everyone at the table has wine and a plate full of food, Lucia and Mario take their seats at opposite ends of the table.

"We like to give thanks before we eat." Lucia folds her hands and bows her head.

I notice every head at the table lowers, so I do the same and squeeze my eyes closed. I hope I'm not expected to say anything or hold hands or any of that. I'm not from a religious family, and I don't know any formal prayers.

I'm lost in my thoughts, staring at the steaming heap of food on my plate, when for some reason, I look up. I feel someone watching me, and in spite of the nervousness twisting in my belly, I chance a look at Franco.

It's him.

He's watching me.

Staring at me.

I press my lips in what I hope is a reassuring smile and look away.

"And we're so very thankful for our new friend in Chloe." Lucia finishes her prayer, and around me, everyone lifts their glass of wine.

"*Salud*," Benito says, tapping the rim of his glass to his father's.

Everyone around the table echoes the toast, and I

just lift my glass silently and take a sip when everyone else does.

When the meal finally starts, that's when the real awkwardness begins.

"So, Chloe," Lucia starts.

"Ma, for fuck's sake…" Franco has pulled a piece of actual string from the rolled meat on this plate and slices into it with a bang of cutlery against stoneware.

"Franco." It's his father who responds, giving his son a dark look. "We're at the table, son. Language."

Gracie settles back in her chair, a smug look on her face, while Benito grabs the bottle of wine and tops off his glass.

"Would you all just settle down?" Vito, the quietest of the Bianchis, is swirling a forkful of pasta in the air. He looks at me with a warm smile, and I can't help but relax a little.

I look down at my plate piled high with hot, delicious-smelling food.

"Have you ever had braciole before?"

I assume the question is for me. I look up and feel every eye at the table on me. I grab the glass of wine and take a swig, then shake my head. "No, we, uh… No."

Lucia gets all excited at that. "Mario's is the best," she explains, but then she looks at Benito. "No offense, son."

Benito is chewing a mouthful of salad and shrugs.

"It's just beef, dear, rolled into a cute little shape

57

with a filling inside." Lucia is watching me with something so kind and warm on her face, it breaks my heart into little pieces.

She sincerely wants me to eat and like the food. Even if she also sincerely wants me to date her son—and I think by now we all know that isn't going to happen—she's welcoming and warm. She reaches across the table and rubs Vito's arm, urging him to show me how to eat it.

"Ma, stop hovering. You're making *me* nervous. You expect the woman to eat while you're obsessing over every bite?" Gracie is seated next to me, and all three Bianchi sons are across from us on the other side of the table. Gracie takes her braciole in her fork and shows me how to remove the string. "It's just butcher string," she tells me. "Totally sanitary and safe to cook with. It's not like Dad has a sewing kit in the kitchen he uses to wrap up meat with."

I laugh nervously and way too loudly at that, but Mario and Lucia chime in and chuckle. I avoid looking across the table at any of the Bianchi boys and copy what Gracie did, unwrapping the string from the beef.

I don't even need a knife to cut into the thin, tender, rolled strip. I take a bite and widen my eyes, looking from Gracie to Mario. "Holy crap," I gasp as soon as I swallow. "That is…" I'm searching for the right word, while Mario waves a hand at me.

"If you don't care for it, don't eat it." He's trying to be nice, but I'm not.

"No," I say over him, finding my voice. "This is exceptional. I mean, like, the most delicious thing I've ever eaten. It tastes like…"

"Home?" Lucia offers. She sighs and leans back in her chair. "I knew you'd love it. Braciole was your aunt's favorite."

Gracie swirls a forkful of pasta against the inside of a large spoon and cocks her head my direction. "Do you have any brothers or sisters?"

This question gets the whole table's interest. I avoid the stares of the handsome trio across from me and look down at my food.

"You can have half of mine," Benito blurts, laughing at his own joke. "I don't even care which two."

Vito slugs his brother on the shoulder and calls him an asshole, which prompts a whole new round of scolding about language from Lucia and Mario.

"Let her answer," Mario says, shaking his head. "But yeah, if you want one of these knuckleheads, help yourself. You should probably take the one with the smart mouth."

"What did I do?" Gracie blurts before Mario can point to which of his knuckleheads has the smart mouth, and everyone is laughing, even me.

When the giggles calm, I shake my head and answer her. "I don't," I said. "Only child."

They receive that news like I've just said my puppy had been run over by a car, so I can only hope no one asks about my parents.

Alcoholic, abusive dad. Depressed nurse mom... Yeah, I've got all the fun stories when you start to dig for them.

Instead, I decide to turn the tables. "What about you?" I ask, turning to look at Lucia. "Did you and Mario always want a big family?"

Lucia starts talking about how she and Mario are both from big families, but as she speaks, I look down at my plate and spear the last bite of my beef.

I can't help but peek at Franco. He's like the sun, and I'm a seedling just yearning to soak up some of his life-giving strength.

My heart rate speeds up when I see he's watching me, chewing slowly and deliberately, his intense blue eyes locked on me.

Under his hot gaze, I shift uncomfortably in my chair and look away. I hurry to chew my last bite of braciole while Lucia finishes her story.

"After all of that, none of these idiots are mine. They're all adopted."

"You wish," Benito says. "You have no one out there to blame for how we turned out. This is all you and Dad."

The table has turned rowdy and loud, but that's fine with me. No one is asking me any more questions, instead focusing on Benito's restaurant, Vito's job at the fire station, and the latest drama at the animal shelter where Lucia volunteers.

When Gracie gets up to start clearing her plate, I

jump up to help, but she stops me with a hand. "Please," she says. "You're our guest." She takes my plate from me, and as I sit back down, I feel it.

I feel him.

Franco's eyes are following my every move. I swallow back my nerves as a little zing of electricity brings my body to life.

My belly is warm and full, but there's a different kind of pleasure when I feel Franco's eyes on me. He looks away when my eyes meet his, and I wipe my clammy hands on my thighs.

The meal was delicious, and the company—once they stopped talking about me—was a little overwhelming, but honestly so much fun.

During dessert, Vito excuses himself to bed. He apologizes that he's got to sleep at odd times due to his shifts at the firehouse, and after kisses to his parents and a sleepy nod at me, he's gone.

Even with one fewer Bianchi at the table, the conversation is no less animated. I listen in and savor the gooey, buttery cake that pairs perfectly with the strong coffee.

As he's shoveling the last bite of cake into his mouth, Benito slaps a hand on the table and leans over to kiss his mother. "Dinner was amazing. Love you all. Got to run. Got to get back to work."

He doesn't bother to clear his plate, and Franco and Grace both sigh and roll their eyes.

Mario gets up to give his son a hug, and Benito

waves at me. "Nice to meet you, Chloe," he says. "I'll treat you to some real Italian cooking if you come down to my restaurant."

That elicits an outburst of good-natured insults from the family, and in a flash, Benny is out the door.

Franco jumps up and clears his brother's plate.

I get up to do the same, but again, Grace stops me. "Sit," she says, waving a hand at me. "Relax."

I'm pretty sure if I stay any longer, avoiding Franco's eyes like they are lasers waiting to cut into my soul, I won't be able to relax for days.

I'm ready. It's more than past time to go.

"I'd better head home," I say. "I walked, and it's getting pretty late."

Turns out that is the absolute wrong thing to say.

"You what?" Lucia is abuzz with nervous energy, her pretty face pulled into a strained scowl. "What's wrong with your car? You have a car, don't you, honey? What happened to that little sedan you were driving?"

I shrug. "It's fine. I just… It was a beautiful day, and I thought I'd walk."

That's not true, of course. But the last thing I want to get into is the fact that I'm so broke I don't even have gas money at the moment. I mean, I did… I just chose to put the little money I did have into other things. There's no point in these people getting all worried or worked up about my choices.

Mario shakes his head. "No, no, that's no good. Where do you live? I'll take you home."

That starts the fight of the century—or at least it sounds like it.

Lucia is giving him the area I live in and exclaiming that I must have walked three miles to get here.

Mario pushes back from the table and tugs his glasses over his eyes while he punches my address into his phone. "Is that it? I've been meaning to try this new map app my kids put on my phone. I used it the other day to drive into Cleveland. Worked pretty good."

I bite back a smile and hold up my hands. "Please," I say. "It's okay. I've eaten enough to fuel me for a marathon. I'll be just fine."

"Oh no, you won't." Lucia is acting like I've suggested I swim across Lake Erie nude in January. "And Mario, you've had two glasses of wine. You're not driving anybody anywhere." I follow her finger with my eyes as she points at her son. "Franco, you're driving home anyway. You can take Chloe home on the way."

"Oh no, I… It's okay. I…" The words die on my lips as I meet Franco's stony stare.

He looks annoyed, exhausted, and like he fully expected me to pull a trick like this. He probably thinks his mother and I schemed this up just as a way to get the two of us alone.

All of a sudden, all the food in my stomach isn't sitting so well. "Really, I don't want to be any trouble." I push back from my chair and head to Lucia. The last thing I want is to ruffle anyone's feathers. Especially her son's. "The meal was amazing," I tell her, tentatively opening my arms for a hug.

Lucia pulls me close and holds me tight. "You're never alone, you hear me?" she asked. "You have family here, Chloe." She kisses my cheek and releases me, shouting for her husband to hurry up and make me a plate of leftovers.

"Oh no, I…"

"It's pointless." Franco's grumpy rasp sends chills along my arms. Even under my thick cardigan, I can feel every inch of my skin pebble as though a cool breeze is blowing right through every layer I have on.

I turn slowly and face his searing gaze. "I'm sorry? I…"

He holds up a hand. "You're not going to win this one. Ma will have visions of you dying by serial killer all night, so you're not going to walk home. And Dad won't stop complaining that you didn't like his cooking if you don't take a plate." He crosses his arms over his chest. "You may as well get your boots on. As soon as your leftovers are ready, I'll drive you."

He stalks up to the front door, where his boots are waiting beside mine. I keep my eyes on the floor as he walks past, hoping he won't see I'm embarrassed by every bad choice I've made that's led me to this moment. The outfit I wore, the boots, walking here. I've never felt more wrong or unsettled within myself.

I squeeze my eyes shut and lean against the wall with my back to him as I slip on my boots.

I'll be home soon. Done with this night that I can file away as a wonderful memory of something I never have to go through again.

Once my feet are securely in my boots, I look back over the Bianchi home.

Gracie and Lucia have cleared almost all the dishes, and Mario is coming from the kitchen with a heck of a lot more than a plate. He's packed up a travel bag of some kind. He's easily got several pounds of food in there by the size of it.

"Pops, she's one person." Franco reaches his hand to take the handle of the travel container.

Mario lifts a shoulder. "And now she won't have to cook for herself for a while."

"That's too much," I say, shaking my head. "Too generous."

Mario waves me off with a hand. "Come anytime, sweetheart." He gives me a grin and then turns to his son. "Get her home safe, and then yourself." He claps Franco on the shoulder, and Franco gives his dad a kiss on the cheek.

"Thanks for dinner, Pops. Love you. Love you, Ma. I'm leaving!" Franco bellows through the house, and I hear Gracie come padding into the hallway.

"She's up to her elbows in soap suds. She says bye and she loves you." Gracie kisses her brother's cheek, then smacks him hard on the back. "Don't be a dick," she says, and Franco glares.

"Bye, sweetie," Gracie says to me. "I'll probably see

you Tuesday for coffee." She leans in and gives me a kiss on the cheek, and I'm so stunned you could probably knock me over with a feather.

I nod and say nothing, just look back at the dogs on the couch, the table that's almost completely clear of dishes, and I can hear the sounds of water running far off in the kitchen.

I was so anxious to get home, but now that it's time to leave, a part of me feels rooted to the floor.

This is a home.

A real family.

So unlike anything I've ever had, and while it was a lot at first, I'm already sort of adjusting to it.

But then Franco clears his throat and opens the front door.

"Did you bring your bike?" Mario asks, peering past him toward the street.

"Nah," Franco says. "Drove the truck. We'll be fine." He lifts a thick brow at me. "You ready?"

And even though I'm not at all sure that I am, I nod and follow Franco and ten thousand pounds of leftovers out into the night.

The drive is only three miles, but somehow walking it seemed to feel faster than riding beside Franco.

He hasn't said a word since we got inside, other than to ask for my address. He opens his window and then mine just a crack. He leans his elbow out the window, resting it on the door, and drives with one hand. He seems completely at ease with the silence.

For the first few minutes, I am too, but then it just gets weird.

"So, Franco." I force myself to say his name. It feels dangerous and delicious on my lips, and I shake my head to clear away the idiotic thoughts. "Are you a reader?" I ask.

"What?" His question is sharp-edged and defensive.

"Read?" I press. "You know, I own a bookstore now. I was just curious if you, you know…read."

I watch him out of the corner of my eye and see his shoulders relax just a little. "Oh," he says. "Nah. I'm not much for books."

"Ouch," I say, clutching my heart. "I think that brings me actual physical pain."

"Could be heartburn from the coffee and sauce," he says, and something in his voice is a tiny bit lighter.

Is he *teasing* me?

I let myself relax into a full smile. "No, no, I'm pretty sure what I feel is my little bookselling heart breaking. Have you always been that way? Or did you just kind of stop reading after you got out of school?"

He flicks a quick glance at me. "That way?" he echoes. "You make it sound like I'm defective."

Oh boy.

The momentary lightness between us has just been obliterated.

Nice one, Chloe.

I slide my hands back into the sleeves of my sweater and wrap my wool-covered fists together. "That came out wrong. Sorry," I say quietly. "Just trying to make conversation. But we don't have to talk. I appreciate you being willing to give me a ride."

I lean a little closer to the passenger side window and stare out into the town that rolls past. I notice plenty of trees in Star Falls, lovely houses, and well-tended lawns. I entertain myself by counting the number of pickup trucks we pass.

I've just counted five when Franco blurts out, "So what's the real reason you walked? Something wrong with your car?"

I definitely can't tell him the truth, but I also don't want him to look at it and realize I'm just about out of gas. He'll either think I'm really stupid, or he'll think I'm pathetic.

"It was stupid of me. I should have driven. I thought the walk would be nice." I'm staring out the window, watching the blocks pass, wishing the longest car ride I've ever been on was almost over.

With every breath I take, the truck seems to be warmer, and a mouth-watering fragrance that has to be Franco competes with the food. A light hint of smoke and oil and...I don't know what it is, but it smells like warm leather and sunshine.

I wish I could lean into his neck and take a deep breath, and yes, that officially makes me creepy.

I can't help it.

He's the kind of man that any woman would want to lean into and smell.

"I don't have anything against books," he says, returning to our previous conversation, thankfully unaware of the deep breaths I'm taking as I pull in his scent. "I do read. I shouldn't have said that before. I mostly read nonfiction and shit online. That's what I meant."

A bloom of heat unfurls in my chest. He's trying to be kind. He's trying to open up a little. I won't read more into it than it means. I'm just super happy that the weird, awkward bubble stealing all the air between us seems to have popped.

"Awesome," I say, a little too brightly. "I wasn't judging you."

"I don't know about that," he says, his voice a sultry purr. "You just about had a full-on heartbreak when I said I didn't read. I think you *were* judging me." But this time, there's nothing defensive or guarded in his words.

I lean back against the seat and smile. "Hmmm, true. I was judging you harshly. In fact, I was secretly planning to pull my aunt's chicken-and-bacon grilled cheese from the café menu just to punish you."

He chuckles a bit and turns on the blinker as he slows to a stop in front of my building. "This you?" he asks.

"Yep." I unfasten my seat belt and pull on the door

handle. I open the door just a crack, but I don't step out just yet.

The silence is back between us, the air in the truck thick with tension. I feel like I can't leave without saying something, without addressing it somehow. It's not my fault his mother wants to set us up any more than it is his. And I just don't think I can be friends with Lucia if Franco is constantly...mad like this. Or whatever this is.

"Franco," I say.

He doesn't face me but stares straight ahead. "You're welcome. Have a good night."

He's not even going to look at me. In his mind, he's already left, maybe planning wherever he's off to next.

A woman's place, maybe? Yeah. He's probably got a lot better places to be than with me.

But something inside me doesn't want to be ignored. Dismissed. I pull the door closed and turn fully in my seat to face him.

"Thanks for this." I rest my hand lightly on his arm.

He tenses under my touch and turns toward me.

The engine is idling, and we're parked just below a streetlamp.

He is bathed in artificial light, making shadows fall over the sharp planes of his face. His eyes, even in the darkness, are intense as he just watches me. Waits.

I yank my hand back as if he's burned me, but I don't look away. Something about him makes me want to be bolder. Stronger. I want him to see me. Who I really am, not the needy wannabe date that his mom's made me out to be.

"I just want you to know that I'm not in on whatever plan or scheme your mom has going on. I don't want her to set me up with you. I mean, I had no idea that was on her mind. I just... I mean... You're... You know..." All of a sudden, this definitely feels like high school. I have no clue what to say, and yet words keep coming, spilling past my lips and fighting one another as they come out.

Franco is looking at me with a combination of confusion and something else... Amusement, maybe? I don't like it, and I can already feel the flush burning its way up my chest and leaving a feverish heat in my cheeks.

"I'm what?" he asks quietly.

"Excuse me?" I'm blinking and leaning away from him, but he's leaning toward me. The beam of ugly light from the streetlamp falls over his features as he looks at me.

Really looks at me.

Suddenly, I'm speechless. My body feels warm; my hands shake. With every breath, I smell leather and smoke and pasta sauce, and the truck cab feels suddenly way too small to contain the energy, the whatever this is that I'm feeling. I'm quiet as I fumble behind me for the door handle.

"You said that I'm something, but you didn't finish. So, what is it? What am I?" He shocks the heck out of me by reaching forward and tipping my chin up with two fingers.

His skin is hot and surprisingly rough and soft at the same time, and a bolt of electricity shoots through my limbs. I gasp a little, deep in my throat, and lick my dry lips.

Franco drops his hand and glares again, and I shake the moment off. Whatever that was, that chin-touch thing…it felt good. Too good. Like, I'm hot between my legs, and I'm going to ride my vibrator tonight thinking about those long, strong fingers. His intense blue eyes.

The stubble on his chin rough against my…

Oh hell.

The fact that I'm in a enclosed space with this man thinking about getting myself off to his fingers…

This night has officially gotten out of control.

"I'm going to go in," I blurt out in a rush. "I just wanted to clear the air." I scramble toward the door and practically fall onto the sidewalk.

I smooth down my sweater, trying to fix how I look on the outside in case I look as jumbled up and wild as I feel inside. I fumble for my keys, keeping my chin down.

No matter what, I'm not looking back.

He waits there, idling, until my trembling fingers unlock the dead bolt and the doorknob—two separate locks, and even with just one key, it feels like so many extra steps—and then I open the front door.

I flip on the hall light so he can see I made it inside

and there are no killers waiting in the shadows. Once I'm inside, I lock the knob and dead bolt behind me, and then finally the headlights of his truck pull a U-turn in the street, and he drives back in the direction we came.

My heart is beating way too fast, and I've broken into a light sweat. I kick off my boots and head straight for the bathroom.

"That's it," I say. I knot my hair in a bun on the top of my head and dig in the bathroom vanity for my vibrator.

But then I shake my head and put the plastic toy back under the sink.

A bath and a steamy book are the only cure for these feelings.

Because for better or worse, I've got a pickup truck-sized crush on Franco.

CHAPTER 5
FRANCO

"YOU GOING to Latterature for some food?" When my buddy Jack shouts over the music, my heart stops for a second, like I've been caught stealing.

Which I kind of was.

I still haven't found the damn purchase order Jack lost last week, but instead of digging through yet more piles of paperwork, I'd been staring off into space. Lost in a filthy fantasy about the owner of Latterature.

Ever since last night when I spent, what, ten minutes alone in my truck with the woman, I haven't been able to stop thinking about her.

She's nothing, and I mean *nothing*, like the women I usually go for. And that might be what had me fisting myself in the shower this morning.

"What?" I growl, half pissed that I've been interrupted, half embarrassed.

"I thought you were going to run over there." Jack's

still working on the town car, and I've made zero progress on the paperwork. "You said you had to bring her leftovers she forgot?" Jack slides out from under the town car and wipes his hands on his coveralls. "Dude, she forgot it. I call dibs on Mario's cooking."

Normally, I'd agree with Jack. You snooze, you lose. But after Chloe hustled out of my truck last night and left the food my dad had packed behind, I figured bringing it to her would be the right thing to do. At least, that's what I've been telling myself all day.

"I don't know who would be more pissed at me, my mom or my dad," I say. "What's up with Carol? She sick of making you lunch?"

Jack's face darkens, and he gives me a one-armed shrug. "It's weird, man." He looks over his shoulder like his old man is going to walk through the door any second. But he's not.

Jack's dad took a fishing trip two weeks ago when his wife asked for a separation and moved out. The separation shocked me, but Jack has been lost without them.

"What's weird?" I press. "I mean, other than everything going on in your life right now. No offense."

He shakes his head. "None taken." He sighs and yanks off the cap he likes to wear over his wild Irish hair. "I know my parents are separated and shit, doing their own things, but like...my mom didn't come home last night."

My gut tightens, and I'm up out of my chair at the

first hint that anything could be wrong with one of my mom's friends. "You hear from her?" I demand. "Is she staying with Sassy or Bev?"

Jack holds up the hand that grips his cap and sighs. "She's all right. I knew she wasn't coming home. She texted me last from…" He curls his mouth into a frown and mutters something under his breath.

"What? What the fuck, you got me worried. What's up with Carol?" I press, not quite ready to drop down into my chair, not quite convinced that my best friend's mom doesn't need us to do something, go someplace.

"She spent the night at Ray Morris's." Jack says the words like he's got a gun to his head, his teeth gritted to hold in the truth against his will.

My shoulders immediately sag in relief. But only for a second. "Fuck." I swallow back the words I want to say and try to think of a way to be supportive.

Jack's parents have been separated for just a few weeks. If Carol's having sleepovers with other men while his father's out finding himself on the lake…

"Fuck," I say again, and Jack nods.

"Yeah. So, Ma didn't make me lunch, but she's making it for somebody."

Jack looks so heartsick, I can't even chuckle. It sucks. My parents have been together since they were teenagers, and they still seem to feel like the sun rises and sets for their love alone.

"I'm sorry. It's a shit situation all the way around."

Jack nods, slips the cap back over his head, and

shakes his head slowly. "I just keep asking myself what's my place here, you know? Should I tell my dad that Mom's out there getting her rocks off? Warn him before he gets home and finds out from someone else?"

I have no clue what to say to that. I mean, he's not wrong. If Carol's banging Ray, it's probably already front-page news. Not a whole lot stays secret in a small town.

"I wish I could help you, man." I feel useless and helpless. I hate that feeling. "If we were twenty years younger, I'd say let's go kick Ray's ass," I say unhelpfully.

It does get Jack to chuckle. "Thanks. I don't think Ma would be too happy about that. She seemed happy last night. When she texted, I mean."

"That's a good thing, right?" I'm grasping at straws here. I mean, Ray Morris has got to be in his mid-sixties. Would I really go kick his ass if Jack asked me to?

Jack nods and sighs again, the long sigh of a man who sees the reality before him but hates that he's powerless to change it. "That's what matters, right? That she's happy? Even if it breaks my dad's heart."

We're both silent then. What else is there to say?

"If Ray hurts your mom, I'll be the first one to go down there and beat the guy's ass. And when your dad gets back, if he's, you know…devastated… He's got you. He's got the shop. He'll be okay. And you never know. Sometimes the grass is greener, but your mom and pop have been together a long time."

Jack looks sad then. Sadder than I think I've ever seen him. "I know," he says. "That's why I'm pretty sure this is a permanent thing. Neither one of them has been happy for a long time."

He gets back underneath the town car but calls out, "If you change your mind, I'm down for a plateful of Mario's cooking for lunch. No pressure, fucker."

I chuckle and shake my head. "Those are spoken for, but how's about this? I'll treat you to dinner at Benny's place tonight. Go home, change into something respectable, and drop me a text when you're ready. I'll pick you up and drive. Cool?"

"Thanks, man."

He gets back to work, and I'm back to my endless, pointless, meaningless review of Carol's paperwork.

But I think about his parents and how lost Jack will be if they do split up. Will Carol quit her job at the shop? All of a sudden, this project I'm working on seems a lot less meaningless.

All afternoon, I told myself I was waiting to go to Latterature until after work because I had a lot to do. The truth is, I was putting it off.

By the time the sky turns purple and dark gray

clouds are skating trails across the horizon, Jack's finished the town car.

"You feel up to a trip to The Body Shop?" Jack calls over his shoulder as he washes his hands in the shop sink.

"You want a tattoo?" I ask, stunned. "I mean, my sister can probably hook you up, but you usually need an appointment. They book out like weeks or more, and it's closed tonight anyway."

Jack shakes his hands dry since we're out of paper towels—another thing that Carol handled when she worked here—and laughs. "No, man. I'm talking the strip club."

Of course the only strip club in the county has the exact same name as the only tattoo shop in the county. Michelle, my brother's ex-wife, met him at the "other" Body Shop. The one Jack's talking about now.

"Nah, I'm not in the mood for a lap dance. We can rain check dinner, though, if you'd rather have some tits in your face." I pull the insulated food bag out of the office fridge, which desperately needs a cleanout.

As we lock up and head to the parking lot, Jack claps me on the back. "Thanks for the offer. Let's grab a nice dinner another time. I think tonight I want some loud music, watered-down drinks, and something soft grinding on my lap."

I nod and wave to him. "Have fun. Be safe out there. If you see Exotic…" I lift my brow at him and try not to burst out laughing.

Michelle, also known as Exotic, was Jack's favorite dancer until she married my brother.

"She's not getting a goddamn thing from me."

"Good man." I laugh.

Jack flips me the finger, but then drives off in his antique truck. I pull out not long after him but find every excuse in the book not to go straight to Latterature.

I stop and fill the truck with gas, carefully cleaning the windows, even though the truck is perfectly clean. I head into the gas station and make small talk with the girl at the counter before finally getting my ass in gear.

I start up the truck and head toward downtown. Worst case, if she's not there, I can drop by her place.

It occurs to me, of course, that maybe that's the real reason I'm stalling going to the shop.

Am I hoping to miss her at the café?

Looking for a reason to go back to her tiny apartment, walk the steps, and show up at her door bearing food?

"Fuck me sideways," I grumble to myself. I'm acting like a damn kid. I smooth my hair in place and angle the truck down nearly deserted Main Street.

It's past six by the time I roll up to the shop. I decide to drive past to make sure she's still there before I bother parking.

I squint as I pass to see if maybe Chloe left a light on, or if she's still back there. Maybe working in the kitchen.

The street is deserted, and something in my gut just feels off. This isn't butterflies or awkwardness about showing up with the forgotten food either.

I don't know what this is.

But in true stalker style, I darken my lights and creep past the café, feeling a mix of concern and shame.

This is normal.

Totally normal.

As I come close enough to the shop to see inside, I spot Chloe standing in the middle of the store. My shoulders relax a little, but then I see her holding her hands up in a weird way—almost like she's at gunpoint.

It can't be.

I slam on the brakes, but the truck doesn't make a sound. I squint to try to make out what's going on, but I can't see anyone else in the café. She can't be standing like that for no reason, and something inside me panics.

Adrenaline fires in my gut, and my pulse starts thundering. Before I even have time to think, I'm turning the wheel of the truck, and I pull over on the opposite side of the street.

I run at full speed across the street, propelled by anxious energy and a suddenly desperate fear that my instincts were right.

I'm a big, strong guy, but if there's somebody armed in there…

Fuck.

I don't have a plan, just a frantic need to get into the

store and make sure my mind's just playing tricks on me.

I didn't see what I thought I saw.

But when I get to the front of the store, it becomes obvious I saw exactly what I thought. A dark figure with a mask over his face and his head down comes barreling through the front door.

I see him coming, and I stand with my feet braced, knees bent, ready to fucking tackle his ass.

He seems as shocked to see me as I am to see him.

He stops, pants a little, and grunts in a voice that sounds fake-low, "Get the fuck out of the way before I fuck you up."

"I'm going to fuck you up, you piece of shit." I lunge to tackle him, but the asshole is skinny, and he rolls to one side like he's been dodging the law his whole life.

I grab for a handful of his hoodie and get a decent grip on it. The guy knows he's about to get caught, and he is wiggling and kicking like a trapped wild beast.

For some reason, the dude isn't punching me, isn't doing anything but trying to wrestle away from the fistful of hoodie that's slipping through my fingers.

I'm able to land a couple punches to his head, but they don't slow him down. He's wiry as fuck. He grunts and cusses me out with each blow.

He drops a plain blue zipper bag, the exact same kind that Jack uses to take cash into the bank.

He was fucking robbing the store.

My vision goes red.

I scream, a primal, murderous sound, but the guy knows that I'm big and now very pissed off.

Without a second look at the bag he dropped, he takes off running at full speed.

I debate following him, but it's pretty clear I'm not likely to catch him. He's dressed for escape, and I'm in steel-toe work boots.

My heart is throbbing in my chest as I reach down and grab the blue money bag from the ground so the fucker can't run back and get it.

I yank open the door and start shouting, "Chloe! Chloe!"

I find her exactly where I'd seen her as I crept down the street. But she's not standing. She's lying in a heap on the floor with her eyes closed.

"Chloe!" I yell again and drop to my knees. I fumble in my pocket for my phone and dial the cops, and with my other hand, I reach down and press a hand to her cheek.

She's ice-cold.

By the time I explain to the dispatcher what's happened and give her the pathetic bits of description I can about the thief, Chloe starts to wake.

"Hey, hey," I say softly as a sense of relief washes over me. I've got one hand on my cell phone, and with the other, I stroke her hair away from her face. "Stay with me. An ambulance is on its way."

She blinks very slowly, but within a few seconds,

the color returns to her face and she sits up. "Oh my God," she whispers, and before I know it, she's retching on the floor.

"Chloe," I say, keeping my voice as gentle as I can. "Did he hurt you? Are you hurt?"

I can hear the police sirens in the background, and the dispatcher is telling me the police are less than a minute away.

"She's up," I tell dispatch, but she doesn't want me to end the call or disconnect until EMS arrives on the scene.

"Is the door unlocked?" the lady on the other end of the phone asks. "They'll break down the door if they can't get in."

"Yeah, yeah, I'll meet them. Don't let them go busting in the door," I mutter, because now that Chloe is conscious—shaking and crying but conscious—the only thing I give a shit about is making sure she's okay.

"Chloe," I say again quietly. "Are you hurt?"

She doesn't respond.

I hear the squad car slamming its doors out front. I bark into my phone that the police are here and I'm hanging up. I toss my phone on the floor, then run to the front doors to greet the officers.

The squad car has its lights going, and before the officers even reach the store, an ambulance pulls up and parks.

"She was passed out when I came in," I say to the paramedics. "She woke up, puked, and hasn't moved or said a word. I don't know what happened in here. All I know is what happened out on the street."

The officers ask me a few questions about the details, what I saw, what I remember about the clothes, the body size, anything I can tell them about the guy. But unfortunately, it's just not much. With the mask and hoodie, I couldn't tell them if he was pink, purple, or anything else.

"It happened so fast," I say. "I didn't get a look at his hands, but he must have had gloves on. I would have remembered if there was any skin showing. I don't even remember the color of his eyes. I'm sorry. I just... I... Can we do this later?"

My heart is finally starting to slow down, and the only thing I care about is checking on Chloe. The paramedics already walked past me and are talking to Chloe. I am still giving the police my statement when one of the EMS lifts his head and calls over to me.

"Hey, Franco. Can you come back here?"

I recognize the guy as one of my brother Vito's buddies. "Hey, Nick." I look at the cops. "Am I good here? Can I go?"

They let me go back into the store, so I walk over to Nick.

"Is she okay?" I ask. I could ask Chloe herself, but she's shaking so hard that the other paramedic has her sitting on the floor while he asks quiet questions and checks her out.

"Pretty sure it's shock," Nick tells me. "She's going

to need a bit, though. I'd be scared out of my ass too. The guy had a knife. From what it sounds like, it was a big one—hunting style. You were both lucky no one was hurt."

Before I know it, I'm stalking past Nick, shoving my way past the other paramedic, and I'm on my knees on the carpet in front of Chloe.

"Hey," I whisper. "You're okay. It's going to be okay now."

She looks up at me and swallows. She blinks, tears streaming down her face, and throws herself into my arms.

CHAPTER 6
CHLOE

"ARE THOSE MINTS?" My voice is unnaturally hoarse from all the heaving and crying. "Can I have one?"

I'm in the passenger seat of Franco's truck, and as soon as I see the tin of mints in the center console, I think about my puke breath and my parched throat.

"Yeah. Help yourself." Franco has been quiet on the drive, but to be fair, I have been too.

We spent more than two hours with the police at Latterature. Plenty of time for me to go over what happened.

Again and again.

Too many times, it seemed.

And no matter how many times I explained it, it was never less terrifying.

The guy was quiet and forceful, like he'd done this

before and knew exactly how to use my shock against me.

I did as he asked, pulling out the blue zipper envelope that my aunt used to make her bank deposits. I put what little cash we had in the bag.

The guy grabbed the pouch and made me hand over my cell phone. He told me to count to two hundred, and then, he said, I could call the cops. But he said if I followed him or tried anything, that he would *fillet* me.

Those were his words.

I told the police exactly what he'd said, and they traded a look, like maybe it was something they'd heard before.

My worries race through my mind as I crunch mindlessly on a mint. The sweet bite of the candy does nothing to calm my nerves or settle my stomach.

I just can't stop the feelings of panic. I don't think, as long as I live, I'll ever forget that kind of raw fear.

How I'd felt when I'd realized what was happening.

How alone I'd felt.

How terrified.

Even now that I am safe, now that it is truly all over, as the moments tick past, I grow more and more angry.

I just can't stop seeing it. Watching it again and again and going through every little detail.

I must be breathing hard or something, because I feel Franco's hand on my shoulder.

"Chloe?" Franco's voice breaks through the endless loop replaying in my mind.

"Sorry?" I blink and watch his face as he stares at me.

"We're here. Your place."

I realize that we've stopped, and we're parked outside my apartment. That means it is time to go inside alone.

"He has my cell phone," I whisper, a violent shiver shaking my body so hard I can't hide the tremor. "What if he…"

"Come on." Franco leaps out of the truck and comes around to the passenger side. He holds out his hand to me. "I'm going to walk you in, and you're going to pack a bag. You can't stay here tonight. Not by yourself."

I shake my head as the reality of what is happening hits me.

Where am I going to go?

Where can I possibly stay? I can't afford a hotel. I don't have friends in town yet. I've only been in Star Falls a couple of weeks.

All I have is my aunt's apartment and her landline. Maybe one of the ladies would let me crash on her couch, but God, I can't impose.

And even if I could for one night, what then?

Staying here alone while some psychopath has my phone? He didn't get what he wanted from my café. Maybe he'll come back.

The heat of the truck starts to feel stifling, and I break out in a sweat.

"I... I..." I don't know what to do. I can't move. Can't think fast enough.

"Chloe." Franco's voice is raspy, as if he's as worn out as I am. I realize I haven't thanked him. "*Chloe.*" He's saying it again, but this time, he's closer. He's staring at me with those summer-sky eyes, and a weary half smile claims his beautiful mouth. "I'm not going to leave you," he promises. "I'm going to go up with you. You're going to pack a bag, and I'm going to bring you someplace safe. Okay?"

I stare at Franco's outstretched hand. If he'd offered his hand to me yesterday, I would have leaped at the chance to touch him.

Today, holding his hand means I have to move. Have to go inside. Face the reality and fears all alone, even if he walks me as far as the door.

I can't do it.

"I have to go home," I say, quietly wringing my hands.

I can't do any of this.

"You *are* home," Franco says, looking puzzled. He rests a hand on my thigh and gives it a gentle squeeze. "Chloe." His voice is a lifeline. Warm, steady, and solid.

Gone is the broody grump who wouldn't look at me over dinner or who glared at me for too long.

This Franco is nothing if not sincere.

"I'm right here. Come on. Let's go inside. I won't let anything hurt you. You got that? I'm right here. And I wish

I'd fucking been there at the store five minutes earlier." He squeezes his lips together and flares his nostrils. But then he releases my thigh and clicks open my seat belt. "Take my hand. Let's get a bag packed and get the fuck out of here."

He eases my seat belt away from my body, and now there is nothing left to do but take his hand and move one leg at a time out of the truck.

The fall air is crisp, and his breath curls in front of his face in soft puffs of steam. My hand shakes as I reach for his. My legs feel weak but also like they are surging with fear, like at any moment, I could break into a run and take myself far, far away from here.

The intensity of the experience is too much. I hit the pavement, and my knees buckle. "Whoa." I reach for the truck door, but Franco is there instead.

His body is warm and firm, and he's got a hand on my waist, but somehow my thighs are plastered against his. I follow my body's momentum and lean all the way into him.

"Whoa," he echoes what I just said, but his word is heavy with something else. His breath fans my ear, and for a moment, I get lost in the reassuring comfort of him. He's like a wall of muscle blocking the rest of the world from getting to me.

It's probably the stupidest thing I've ever done, but I lean my forehead against his chest and close my eyes. Maybe I'm chickenshit, hiding like this behind a man I hardly know. But before I can think better of what I'm doing, I lift up on my toes and wrap my arms around his neck.

"Thank you," I breathe against his neck. The long layers of his hair tickle my face, and I'm a little too short to reach comfortably, but he is already wrapping his arms around my waist and pulling me close. I hug him hard and let the tears burn the backs of my eyelids. "What would have happened if you hadn't come when you did?"

I mean, I know the criminal was already outside when Franco arrived, but the guy took my phone. The store has a landline, but I was so weak and terrified.

Would I have been able to call for help? What if I'd passed out alone?

My entire body trembles, and he holds me even closer. The unbelievable heat of him seeps through my clothes, and, if anything, I hold on even tighter.

He doesn't say anything and doesn't relax his hold on me. "I won't let anything happen to you," he promises. "You're okay. You're going to be okay."

I breathe in the heady scent of his hair, the light fragrance of hair oil, soap, smoke, and I know I have to let go. I'm embarrassing myself further. But my body knows what it wants, and this biker-mechanic-body-guard is exactly the shield I need right now. I will rally.

I will get past this. But right now? I'm in no state to pretend to be stronger than I am.

"I don't really want to let go," I admit, my words sounding fuzzy against his collar.

I can feel his hands through my sweater, firm but gentle on my waist. "How about we try this?" he says. "Let's walk inside. Let's get you packed. And then, if you need more of this, you just come on back for more."

I nod and loosen my hands and steady my feet beneath me. I wipe my hands on the legs of my pants and shake clear the cobwebs.

One thing at a time.

"Inside. Pack a bag," I repeat, more to myself than to him, feeling suddenly vulnerable again. There is a clear path between me and the exterior stairs that lead to my apartment. No massive man blocking the way. "Where do you plan to take me? I don't want to impose on anyone, and—"

"My place," he says. "You can stay with me tonight."

Something electric dances in my belly when he says that. In the state I'm in, I can't tell whether it's excitement, relief, or fear that I'm feeling. "Your place?" I shake my head. "You don't have to do that. I can just—"

"Do you want to go stay with my mother?" he asks, no sign of impatience in his voice. Unless I'm mistaken, he sounds tired. "Because if you want to put up with Lucia freaking out and fawning over you, I'll take you straight to my mom's."

The idea doesn't sound half bad, but if the alternative is staying with Franco…

"I don't know," I say, sincerely unsure what I want. "Let's just go inside."

I square my shoulders and head for the stairs, and he calls for me to wait up.

I've only taken a couple of steps, and I freeze in place. He holds out his hand. I give him my keys without a word, and then he takes the lead, heading toward the stairs where he'd watched me walk to my unit last night.

"Which one is yours?" he asks when we get to the top.

The exterior lights are all working, so my number is clearly illuminated. The welcome mat is still Aunt Ann's, a faded sunflower pattern with a happy bee dancing above the petals. I point ahead and tell him the unit, and he nods, then grimly storms toward my door as if expecting to see the intruder waiting there for me.

"Franco," I whisper. There's a lot I don't know about technology, and so I know my question is probably foolish. But I can't help my reactions. It's as if everything inside me is hyperalert, ready to descend into full fight-or-flight at the least sign. "He has my phone. Is it possible for him to find out where I live?"

Franco's plush lips flatten into a hard line, and a dark shadow passes over his bright eyes. "We're not taking any chances." He pulls his cell phone from his jacket pocket and unlocks the device. "The passcode is 0131. For my mother's birthday, January 31." He repeats it, so I'm sure I remember it. "I'm going to go in first. If there's any sign of trouble, you call the cops. All right?"

I nod and nervously hold his phone in a trembling hand. I keep the phone at the ready and watch while Franco sifts through the keys on my ring.

"This one?" he asks.

I nod. "The doorknob takes the same key," I whisper, terrified that the criminal is close by.

It's ridiculous, I know. But I've never been the victim of a crime before. And this was such a close call. He'd brought a knife. What might have made him want to use it? And would he have used it on...me? My vision blurs and I feel dizzy again, but I fight through it. I have to be ready to dial. I have to focus and just trust that I'm safe now. I'm not alone. Franco is here, and any minute now...

"It's all clear, babe. Come on." Franco's face softens, and my tummy flips at the casual endearment. He's inside my apartment now, turning on the hall light.

I follow him in and hand him back his phone. "Thank you," I say. "So, so much."

He closes the door behind me and turns the lock, pocketing his phone and breathing a loud sigh. "Look okay in here to you? Nothing out of place?"

I scan the mildly familiar apartment. Aunt Ann's furniture is all still here. But as my eyes adjust to each light Franco turns on, I feel more and more at ease that nothing has been disturbed. Nothing is out of place.

"It looks okay," I say quietly. My aunt's old refrigerator hums loudly, and for a moment, I want to lie down on the couch and just collect my thoughts. Calm my racing heart and weary nerves.

But Franco has other things on his mind. "Have you eaten?" he asks. "Dinner?"

I scoff and shake my head. "I'll probably never eat again," I say. "Unless some miracle settles my nerves, I'll probably just throw everything right back up."

"My father's leftovers beg to differ." His voice is light, and he nods toward the open bedroom door. "You have a suitcase?"

I search his face, confusion and self-doubt at war in my chest. "Are you sure you want to take me home with you? I mean, you hardly know me, and you've done so much for me already. I don't—"

He stops the words by striding across the living room and lifting my chin with two fingers. His touch is gentle, but the friction of his skin against mine brings every nerve ending to attention.

I raise my eyes to meet his.

"You don't want to go home with me?" he asks.

The question lingers between us, something more than the words he actually asked underlying his meaning.

I swallow and blink, not sure what to do.

If I speak, I'll disturb his touch. If I move, I'll break our safe, gentle connection. My body is insistent in its silence, stillness.

"I do," I whisper, closing my eyes. "But…"

"No buts. It's settled." Franco doesn't release my

face right away, but he smooths the hair back from my face. "Pack what you need for a couple days. I'll be right here."

Then he's gone, his fingers leave my chin and hair, and I'm frozen in place.

He walks to the kitchen and scans the fridge. There are still aged magnets and notes my aunt scribbled when she was alive on the front. I haven't had the heart to move any of her things. I came from Pennsylvania with a carload of clothes, some books, and personal things, but nothing large like furniture.

I'm living a hand-me-down life if there ever was one. And that thought makes the old inferiority swirl up like a tsunami.

I walk to the bathroom and close the door behind me. I drop onto the toilet and let a few quiet tears fall.

Pull up your big-girl panties, I tell myself.

He's a friend. My aunt's friend's son. He's not judging whether or not he wants to date me. He's helping a woman who's gone through a terrifying experience. I'm just lucky it was him who showed up at the café or I might have to spend tonight completely alone.

I dry my tears and twist my hair into a loose bun, then I wash my face with cold water.

"Franco?"

He's standing in the kitchen but starts at the sound of my voice. "What? Are you okay?" he blurts, then comes toward me like he's genuinely concerned some new danger sprung up in my room.

CHELLE BLISS

I'm starting to feel human again, more like myself. I give him a smile. "I just wanted to know if I should pack a pillow and blanket?"

He looks at me with an unreadable expression. His lips are slightly parted, and he seems to notice my hair is up as he trails his eyes from my lips to my hair and back to my face. "No," he finally says. "It's all good. Leave all that, unless you need special things. Ma made sure I have extra of everything."

I shake my head and sling my bags over one shoulder. "I'm getting hungry now, though. I think the shock is wearing off and my survival instincts are kicking in."

He nods. "Good thing I brought Dad's leftovers. We'll eat at my place. You want a drink?"

I nod.

"Just wine, or the harder stuff?" he asks. "I think tonight calls for a gin and tonic."

"I usually stick to one beer or one glass of wine, but I'm up for anything."

I click off the lights and am slightly reassured by how homey the place looks now that I'm calming down. Everything is where it should be. This is where my aunt lived. And this is where I'll make a life too. Tonight is just a scary bump in the new path I'm forging. I'll get through it.

And I'll be okay.

At least, that's what I hope.

CHAPTER 7
FRANCO

WHEN I PULL up to my place, I leave the truck in the driveway but pop the garage door with the opener.

Chloe spent the entire ride looking at her hands and fidgeting in the seat, to the point where she was making me anxious. But something about seeing the lights go on in my garage, along with the sight of my bike, workbench, and weights restores a little sense of normalcy.

I switch off the truck and turn to her. "I'll carry everything. Let's just get you inside."

She mumbles something under her breath and nods, then shoves open the passenger door.

Once we're inside, I lock the garage and set her bags down at the base of the stairs. She has slid out of her boots and is shifting from foot to foot, looking uncertain.

I check the time, and it's nearly nine. I stifle a yawn at the same time my stomach gurgles. "I'm going to heat these leftovers," I tell her. "I've got to cook some pasta, so it might be twenty minutes. That cool?"

She nods. "Can I help?"

"Let's get your things settled, and we'll cook." I grab her bags and bring them upstairs. "I've got shit everywhere," I say, "but you can leave your stuff up here." I drop her luggage and show her the bathroom. "Towels are here. Feel free to shower or take a bath if you want. Just make yourself at home."

She is looking down at her socks, when I realize she might not feel ready to be alone yet. She might want to make a call to someone, but she doesn't have her phone.

"Hey," I say gently, taking a step closer. "Is there someone you want to call? I don't know what else to do here, but you're safe. You can just relax now."

The saddest expression passes over her face before she carefully composes herself.

In that moment, my heart cracks for her.

She looks so young then, younger than a woman who owns her own business and who moved halfway across the country alone should.

"How old are you?" I ask, the words tumbling out before I can stop them.

She lifts a brow at me, but she answers. "Twenty-nine," she says. "Why? How old are you?"

"I'm thirty-eight," I tell her. "And it's nothing. I just… I'm going to make some food."

I turn and clomp downstairs. There's no point in telling her she looks so young I want to physically stop the world from throwing scary shit at her. I can't. I can't protect her, and I don't understand this almost primal instinct in me to do so.

I have a little sister. I've watched Grace go through hard shit, and yeah, I've always been there to back her play. But this feels so very different. So much more complicated. I don't pity Chloe or feel a duty toward her.

I slam my frustration against the kitchen cabinets and fill a pot of water to boil, heavily salting it. I warm the sauce in a pan, adding a little olive oil and water to thin it without changing the flavor too much.

Just after I dump the box of pasta into the stockpot, Chloe pads downstairs. Her hair is damp and is hanging in smooth, combed locks over her shoulders. Little droplets of water drip from the ends and land on a towel she has wrapped over her shoulders like a shawl.

For the many layers of clothes she wears out there in the world, her sleepwear is surprisingly minimalist. She's wearing a pair of soft sleep shorts, emphasis on short, and a loose V-neck T-shirt. Her feet are bare, and I yank my gaze away from her naked legs to pour myself something strong.

"What're you drinking?" I call from the freezer. I drop a generous serving of ice into a glass and set it on the counter. "I've got beer. I can open some wine…"

"Just whatever you're having is fine," she says. She sits at my kitchen table and picks at her nails. "Can I help?"

105

I shake my head and fill a second glass with ice. The pasta's got another three or four minutes to cook, so I grab a lime from the fridge and make us each a strong gin and tonic. I hand her a drink, strain the pasta, and then serve up a plate for each of us.

We eat in silence, and it's almost painfully awkward. I can smell the fresh berry scent emanating from her wet hair, and her face is scrubbed clean but has a lot of the color back in it.

"What did you do back in… Where did you move from? I'm sure my ma told me, but I don't remember."

She nods. "Pennsylvania." She takes a long sip of her drink, and her shoulders relax a little more as she chuckles. "I worked in a bookstore," she says. "But the one back home was a major retail chain. You know the kind—we had an in-store café that was owned by another big company. Having books and a café and running it all myself is quite the change."

"Must be." I've eaten every morsel on my plate, and now I'm feeling it. I'm full and tired. I lean back in my chair and sip my drink. "Are books a thing in your family? Like, did you always know you wanted to own your own bookshop one day?"

I'm slowing down her meal by talking to her, but the silence is too painful. I feel like the less we talk, the more we both get lost in the memories of what happened tonight.

She lets out a laugh and sets down her fork. "Not at

all," she says. "It was actually a huge shock when I learned my aunt left me Latterature."

"Yeah?" I watch her as she talks, checking out the loose curls that are taking shape as her hair dries.

"Yeah," she echoes. "My family wasn't really close to Aunt Ann. Not as close as my mother and I would've liked. I was really shocked she left the place to me. I wasn't sure I even wanted it, but I knew I had to come here and check it out."

Instead of looking away, I watch, a curious heat rising under my skin as I let myself appreciate this woman.

For the first time, she maintains eye contact. "Can I speak freely?" she finally asks.

"That's the only fucking way to do it," I assure her.

"My dad was a drunk," she says simply. "And I know I should be more considerate. He had a disease. An addiction. Alcoholism is no joke, and it's not his fault that he had a problem. But it's hard to separate the man from the booze when the two have such a close relationship."

Hearing that her dad had issues with alcohol makes me sit up a little straighter in my chair, but I don't interrupt.

"My dad never cooked a meal in his life." She chews another bite of pasta and shakes her head thoughtfully. "He sure knew how to scream at me or my mother to bring him dinner, though." She twirls the curly end of a piece of hair between her fingers and looks at me. "My family life was completely opposite of yours. Dad drank and yelled. Mom hid and enabled. And I just tried to stay out of the way."

"In your own family?" I set my glass back on the table, making a louder thud against the wood than I intend. "That sucks," I tell her. "I'm sorry."

I don't know what else to say.

She shrugs and says almost exactly what I'm thinking. "Everyone has problems," she says. "Well, I used to believe that until I met your family. They might just be as close to perfect as I've met."

I snort at that. "We're not perfect."

"Hmmm?" She's got a twinkle in her clear green eyes. "I don't believe you. Sweet, if a little too involved, mother. A dad who cooks and seems doting. Three gorgeous brothers with good jobs and lives, and a sister who, quite honestly, I'm sure most women wish they could be."

When she puts it like that, yeah. We're blessed. I know this. But that doesn't mean we're anywhere near perfect.

"I wonder about that sometimes," I say, realizing a minute too late that she called me and my brothers gorgeous, so I backtrack. "And for the record, I'm the best-looking of the Bianchis. Benito ain't half bad, but Vito…" I shake my head. "Gorgeous he is not."

She laughs. "I don't know," she says, a teasing, playful note in her voice. I like the way the lightness in her tone sounds. "Firefighters are the stuff of romance novels. I would know, I'm a bookseller."

That makes me snort. "Please do not put the image in my head of Vito on the cover of some book."

"Any one of you could be on the cover—not just him," she says, her face flushing. "Let me do the dishes. You've done enough and have been put out too much already."

I hold my hands up in surrender and let her clear my plate. I have a dishwasher, but she takes the towel from around her shoulders and hangs it over the end of the counter to dry.

I can tell she's not wearing a bra under her sleep shirt, and my cock immediately goes to half-mast in my jeans.

Under all those clothes, Chloe has a *body*. Her nipples are hard, the tips pressing against the soft fabric and distracting me from the fullness of her breasts.

Thank God she turns away to rinse the dishes because I'm twitching like a kid who can't resist popping a sheet of bubble wrap. Those tight peaks are all I can think about touching.

I roughly shove my chair back in and try to think about anything else except her nipples. I start talking too, words spilling out of my mouth. "So, you said you weren't sure you wanted Latterature? What are you thinking? You're going to look the place over, fix it up a bit, and sell?"

She shrugs and glances back over her shoulder at

me. "I hadn't made any plans…at least not before tonight."

At the mention of what happened tonight, my belly tightens with a different kind of tension. "And now?" I press.

I shouldn't care what her plans are, but as she stands at my sink in her bare feet, it's impossible not to be curious.

She dries the dishes and turns back toward me. The ends of her hair are hanging over her chest, blocking my view of her more arousing parts.

She smiles, but the gesture doesn't reach her eyes. "I guess I was starting to feel like I could make a life here. Something different from what I had back home. Someplace I might finally belong." A shadow passes over her face, but before I can say anything, she squares her shoulders and puts on a brave smile. "Guess I'm sleeping on the couch?"

"You can take my bed."

She shakes her head. "No. No. I'm not putting you out of your bed. I probably won't sleep much anyway. I'd rather take the couch. Please don't argue with me about this, Franco."

I nod. "I'll grab some clean pillows and blankets." I take the stairs two at a time to burn off some of the electric energy buzzing through my limbs and rummage through my hall closet.

When I'm halfway down the stairs, I see her peering nervously at the sliding glass patio door that leads into the backyard. She moves the curtain aside and checks to make sure it's locked.

"Everything all right?" I ask, and even though she nods, I am not convinced. I start to set out the blankets, a sheet, and two pillows on the couch when she stops me with a hand on my arm.

"It's okay," she says. "You've done enough. Thank you."

I nod and check the front door, garage door, and then the patio slider again so she knows it's all locked up. "Sleep well," I tell her.

I head upstairs but turn back to see her just sitting on the couch, not setting up the bedding. Not moving. She looks up and nods at me, that same artificial bravery plastered on her face.

"Stop," I mutter to myself. "She wants to be alone for a little while."

Post-traumatic stress and my mother's matchmaking ideas are playing tricks with my head.

I stalk up the stairs and into the bathroom. I get ready for bed, then go into my room. But just in case, I climb into bed and leave the bedroom door open.

I don't know what time it is when the noise wakes me, but the telltale creak of the middle stair has me bolting upright in bed.

"Chloe?" The upstairs is dark and the sound stops

when I call her name, so I lie still and listen, my heart rate waking me up faster than I can believe.

I heard something. I know my house, and when I hear it again, that same creak on the stairs, I'm out of bed and at my bedroom door in seconds.

I flip on the hall light and see Chloe looking sheepish. She's on the staircase, her pillows and blankets bundled in her arms.

"What happened?" I blurt, concern overcoming every other emotion. "Are you okay?"

She's paler than she should be, all bare legs and loose hair. "I couldn't sleep down there. I felt too exposed," she explains. "I thought I'd just make a little bed in your guest room."

"On the floor?" I ask because I never bought another bed since I never had a need.

She nods. "Would you mind? I'll be fine." She trudges up the stairs, and I rake a hand through my hair.

"No, no, no," I say. "You take my bed. I've crashed on that couch more times than I can count." I scratch my bare chest and motion toward my room. "Come on. We'll trade."

She looks down at her bare toes, struggling to hold all the pillows and blankets in her arms. "Franco," she says quietly. "Can I stay on the floor in your room? I can't stop seeing him. I can't stop seeing the knif—"

I don't let her finish the word. I take the pillows and blankets from her arms and motion toward my room with my head. She moves past me without looking me in the eye.

I drop the pillows and blankets on the floor, and she leans over like she's about to join them.

"No," I say, shoving aside the pile of blankets with my foot. "Get in the bed."

She looks at me curiously. She doesn't argue, but she also doesn't move.

"Do you trust me?" I ask her as I pull back the comforter and sheet for her.

I know what I'm about to do, and it could go very, very wrong. But I don't care. Whatever my mom saw in Chloe that made her so desperately want to set me up with this woman, I'm seeing it too.

She hums a yes as she slides onto the bed and slips her toes and then her legs under my blankets. I close the bedroom door, then climb into my side of the bed.

We're side by side as far apart on a small surface as two people can be.

"Come here," I say, rolling onto my right side. I hold up the covers, and she scoots closer to me. "I won't bite."

She giggles, which I take as a good sign, and then pushes closer to me. Close enough that I have to sling an arm over her because there is nowhere else for it to go.

"Goodnight, Franco," she whispers. "Thank you."

I tell myself not to. I try to stop myself. But my mouth has a mind of its damn own, and I press a kiss to her hair and nestle my nose deep in the soft, berry-scented waves. "Sweet dreams," I breathe.

She might trust me, but with her body tucked against mine, the curve of her plush ass fitted against my hips, the length of her hair tickling my bare chest, I sure as hell don't trust myself.

CHAPTER 8
CHLOE

I WAKE up cuddled in the most luxurious, comfortable, softest bed I've ever been in. As soon as it hits me that I am not alone in the bed, the fog clears from my mind, and my lids fly open and bug out like a cartoon character's.

The room is dim, the early morning sun still weak behind the blinds. I wiggle my toes, but that's all I dare to move because behind me is a heaping furnace of a shirtless man.

His deep breathing makes me certain he's still sound asleep, but the large palm tucked under my shirt rests against the skin of my belly.

I don't know where his other arm is, but a quick inventory of my body parts confirms it. We're not just spooning. We're nestled like we were made to fit together.

We are tangled up like we've been taking comfort in each other's bodies for years.

We are not just sleeping; we're sleeping *together*.

That we is me...*me*...and Franco Bianchi.

The man who grumped at me the first time we met. Who glared at me across the table through the entirety of my first family dinner.

The weight of Franco's thigh tossed over mine makes me start to sweat. Electric heat sparks beneath my sleep shorts, and I want desperately to rub my thighs together, but I will not budge.

I close my eyes and breathe deeply, but that just makes it worse. The entire bed smells like him. How did I not notice this last night? Yes, I was traumatized and terrified, but I think I could solve all my financial woes if I could just bottle up this scent and put it on the shelves in my aunt's bookstore.

I'd have to call the fragrance Franco, though, because a name like "Italian Working Man" would give off all the wrong vibes.

Okay, it's official. I'm losing my mind.

Last night, I climbed into bed with a man I hardly know, who I thought sort of hated me. Now, I'm lying here wide awake and afraid to move because I don't want to leave the cocoon of comfort and warmth that this man has freely given.

The hard part, and this sobers me up and shoves me halfway out of my sleepy cocoon, is that he's going to wake up and boot me out of his life, probably any minute now.

Deep sigh.

After this morning, I'll cling to this memory for a very long time to come. I hope my vibrator is ready for the floodgates of frustration to open.

I shift a little under the weight of his thigh and scold myself for getting whipped into a lusty frenzy from the smell of his darned sheets, when something happens to correct my thoughts on the matter entirely.

The hard part isn't going to be leaving his bed.

The hard part is actually *in* his bed.

Behind me.

Pressed against my bottom in a way that makes my body do more than just tingle.

My nipples flare to life, tightening into needy, achy peaks. I have to practically bite through my lip to stop myself from thrusting my hips back against him.

How?

How, how, how is this even my life?

I realize in a panic that maybe he isn't asleep, and all the fidgeting, snuggling, and smelling I've been doing have, um, woken him up.

I mean, it's not like he is in this situation because of me. Certainly not *for* me. It's a normal thing that just happens to guys in the morning, but my brazen cuddling is no doubt sending the wrong message.

Or is it the right message?

I don't know, but before I can think myself into a

state of absolute distraction, the hand on my belly tightens and a voice caresses my hair. "Mornin'."

I freeze.

The blood in my body slows down, and I stiffen.

He's awake.

Conscious enough to say words. And his hand hasn't moved, but something south of his waistband twitched a little.

I'm sure that wasn't just wishful thinking on my part. "Good...morning," I whisper back, debating whether to play dead, but deciding against it.

I mean, how the hell are we going to pull ourselves apart from each other?

Better question—how long can I stay this way before I *have* to?

If I have any doubts that Franco knows exactly what he's doing, I feel his hand move from my belly to my ribs, and then finally moves to touch my shoulder.

He pushes the hair back from my face, and I feel him lift his head a little while he smooths the length of it under his head. But he doesn't get up.

He just nestles his head right back where it was, nose resting against my hair. I feel the heat of his breaths against my scalp, and all the little hairs on my arms stand at attention. But not as sharply as my traitorous nipples do.

I suck in a ragged breath of air, the strings of attraction that connect my nipples to my core tightening to a blissful ache.

I'm almost painfully aware of his morning hardness pressing against the crack of my bottom, when suddenly he shifts his hips and moves away, putting just enough distance between us that I can no longer feel his arousal.

Damn.

I don't know what I expected him to do when he woke, but moving away from me was the very thing I didn't want.

When he does, though, I quickly remember that he is who he is, and I'm me.

Plain.

Nerdy.

That gift he is sporting in his pajama pants has nothing to do with me.

"We sure got cozy last night. I hope I didn't make you feel uncomfortable."

My body has clearly taken over my brain because before I can stop myself, I blurt out, "It's what you promised, remember? Self-serve hugs? I wouldn't have stayed here if the damsel-in-distress package didn't come with spooning."

He's quiet for a moment and my cheeks burn hot with mortification, but then a miracle happens. Franco rolls back over and tucks his body tighter against mine. "Is that so?" he growls against my ear.

I press my bottom ever so slightly, so the raging erection he's still sporting is back right where I want it. Well, not *right* where I want it. It's lined up with my butt cheeks.

My hands are itching to reach behind me and touch him, take that length in my hands and guide it where I need it most, but I stop them.

Franco groans under his breath and hisses, but he doesn't move away.

"Thank you," I whisper, then make the painful decision to end this agonizing teasing and roll over to face him before I really embarrass myself.

I inch myself away from his hold, not because it's what I want—because I swear on all that's good and holy, all I *want* is to roll him onto his back so I can mount him until I'm screaming his name. But that's not happening.

Not now, not ever.

Instead, I give myself a mental cold shower and curl onto my side facing him. "I don't think I've ever felt safer or slept better."

"Shit day yesterday. Glad I could help."

"I'm glad too," I admit quietly. "Thank you seems like not nearly enough."

I'm suddenly feeling shy as we look at each other under the covers. The sun is starting to come up, and I can see every muscle in his bare shoulders.

His hair is messy, and the stubble on his chin is thick and delicious. Franco is beautiful. The kind of beautiful that I could lie here and stare at for hours.

"Lots to do today," he says, shoving back the covers.

Those words remind me that this is just a friend

helping a friend. A guy whose mother would guilt him if he didn't offer help. A courtesy.

Thanks to the still-dark bedroom, I'm hoping Franco can't see me watching every flex and stretch of his body as he gets out of bed.

I try to lower my lids so I don't look like I'm checking out his body, but then I give in and just stare. Why not?

My fantasy is ending, and I want to soak up every last second.

Sigh.

He shakes out his shoulders and stretches his arms above his head, and I close my eyes to stop them from rolling as every muscle of his torso moves like a male model warming up before settling into just the right pose.

Come on.

The guy isn't hot enough in clothes, so I've got to watch him shirtless? What next? Is he going to drop and do some crunches?

"You want to shower first?" he asks, breaking in to my thoughts.

I tuck the blankets up to my chin and shake my head. "No, you go ahead. I'll catch a few more minutes of rest."

If lying here and hoping my flaming arousal cools off a little counts as rest, then yes, I will be resting. I'll be resting for at least as long as it takes him to shower.

He nods and rakes a hand through his hair, leaving it

stuck up in the wildest directions, and somehow that's both sexy and cute at the same time.

I consider biting down on the blanket to save my lip from some of the pain, but he closes the bedroom door behind him and I'm alone.

I hear the shower water turn on, and I take one deep breath and savor it. I'm in his bed. My skin still remembers the heat of his hands. This was as close to Franco as I could ever hope to be, and in a few minutes, it will all be over.

I'll be back to my real life, whatever that turns out to be. I'd been so hopeful and open to whatever Star Falls had to offer when I decided to come up here and check out my aunt's café.

But after a night in his arms, the idea of making a life for myself, from scratch, all on my own, no longer feels like such an exciting adventure.

Excitement is what I feel with him, around him. Too bad the only adventure is finding out how many ways a gorgeous, unattainable man can break my heart.

Within the hour, even though I showered last night, I've showered again and joined Franco down in the kitchen. He hands me a mug of hot coffee, and I don't know, but I feel like he's looking at me differently today.

He's got a list written in front of him, and he looks

almost excited to share it with me. I notice he's set a spoon and a sugar bowl on the kitchen table.

"I figured I'd let you put in the sugar for yourself," he says, and then he sits down beside me and starts talking.

I'm looking between him and the spoon and wondering how the heck the man knows I take only sugar in my coffee. But then I realize I had coffee at his parents'. Did he actually pay attention to how I preferred it?

I stir in the sugar and only catch up to Franco's voice when he stretches a hand across the table and rests it on my arm.

"You okay?" He's studying my face. "Did I upset you? Too much?"

Wait, what?

"I was a little lost in my thoughts," I admit. "Sorry. Start over?"

He looks concerned but not angry, which is an upgrade from last week, at least. He points to the hand-written list he's put on the table. "So, I called out of work today. I don't know how you're feeling about going back to the store, but I've made a list of things you probably need to do. We can do them together, or…" He pauses. "Were you feeling up to opening the store today? I sort of assumed you'd want to close the store and…"

"You called out of work?" The sweet coffee is

125

strong, and the way it hits my tongue makes me smile. Or at least, I tell myself it's the coffee.

Franco nods. "I'm fired up as hell. You need a cell phone, and you probably need to check in with your mother," he says. "If something like that happened and I didn't tell my mom for a couple days, she'd..." One side of his mouth curls up. "Well, you know my mother. You know how that would go over."

I nod, but the topic of my mother makes me go silent.

"Hey," he says, a question in his voice. "I'm sorry. Did I touch on something there?"

I shrug, though I don't look up at him. But then I do. Darn it. I'm tired of hiding. Of apologizing for who I am and what my family is—or, more accurately, is not.

"My mother isn't someone I can run to when things happen," I explain. "I wish she were. My whole life, I've held my troubles close to my chest and dealt with them myself. Or maybe not at all. My mom always had enough to deal with just having my dad around. It's a lot easier not to involve her." I give him a weak smile. "I'm only sad about it at the moment because I love what you have with your family. It's the dream, you know?"

Franco doesn't seem to miss a beat. "I know," he says somberly. He takes a sip of his coffee, but his eyes never leave my face. "I know how fortunate I am to have the family I do. I complain about them, but..." He's serious for a moment. "My family is a huge presence in my life. No matter how much I give them a hard time, I live my life with my parents on either shoulder. Most of the time, it's a good thing."

I'm not sure what he means by that, and I want to ask, but he's moved on. I don't want to redirect him. I want to know what he wants to share—and more—so I just listen.

"Ma will be more than happy to panic, freak out, and butt into everything you've got going on. And you've got a whole circle of women desperate to mother you until you feel smothered," he says. "And I'm the oldest of four, so it's just my nature. I'm the bossy older brother."

He jumps up from the table and starts assembling some breakfast. He doesn't ask me what I want; he just cuts up some fruit and starts scrambling eggs.

I'm thrilled because I'm starving, and while his back is to me, I can sort out how I'm feeling.

I realize he's handling me, I guess, like he's my bossy older brother. Except when I think of his hand under my sleep tee, hot against my skin. No. There was nothing brotherly about how he held me last night.

I look over the sheet of paper Franco left on the table. "So, um, what's on the to-do list?" I ask.

"Well, I think, first," he says, "we need to get your phone replaced. And then I was thinking…"

Of course, I hear nothing after that because I have no way of paying for a new phone. The one I had was five years old, so not new by any means but still decent as far as smartphone technology goes.

I wonder if Aunt Ann had insurance on the store. I'm sure she did, but the deductible on policies like that is normally very high. And even if I did make a claim, all that will take more time than I have. How long can I reasonably go without a cell phone?

The coffee starts to sour in my stomach, and I push back from the table. "Franco," I start. "I…"

He sets down the fork he's using to whisk the eggs and looks at me. "What?"

I shake my head. "The phone thing is going to be a problem. I…"

This is all just really, really hard to share. I have such shame around the whole situation.

I need capital. A rainy day fund. And with this unexpected setback? I mean, a serious crime would set anyone back. But I didn't even lose the money in the robbery. Just my phone.

At my age, I should have something in savings and far more than a crap car with no gas in it. And yet, here I am.

"Maybe this is a sign from the universe that I should go home," I say quietly. "That I shouldn't be here. That this is not something I can do."

"Wait, what?" He looks confused. He sets the bowl of eggs on the counter and joins me at the table. "I feel like you're not saying what you're thinking."

I'm standing beside my chair, and he comes closer but doesn't touch me.

Just cocks his chin and narrows his eyes. "Talk to

me, Chloe. What's really going on in here?" He brings his hand to the side of my face. He taps my temple gently with two fingers to emphasize *in here* and then sort of caresses the side of my cheek before dropping his hand to his side. "Sorry," he mutters. "I can't seem to keep my hands off you." He's shaking his head as if he's scolding himself.

"You have an all-access pass," I assure him, flushing hard and laughing. "I'm the one who invited myself into your bed."

He smiles, and his whole face relaxes. He lowers his chin and stares at me, and in that moment, I feel like I'm seeing a whole new side of Franco. Not a more honest side. Because I think he is always exactly who he is.

The grumpy hot guy thing is not a façade or an act, which somehow makes it so much hotter. He's just always himself. At ease in his body and his life and who he is.

It's reassuring to be around, not only because I like who he is, but because I feel somehow like I have permission to just be me. I want to be more like he is in that way.

Honest.

No apologies.

"It's not comfortable to talk about," I explain, trying on this more honest version of myself. "I know I need to replace my phone, but I walked to dinner at your parents' the other night because I'd used most of the cash I had to buy that stupid television. I know it seems like a weird splurge, but I want to start running events at the store. I thought I could... I don't know."

I sigh.

I lift the list and look over the things he's so thoughtfully penned. "A cell phone, a security system..." I swallow and meet Franco's eyes.

I can do this. I can be brave and honest.

"It's all stuff I need, you're right. But I literally do not have the cash."

Franco is quiet for only a split second. "Okay," he says, nodding. "I get it. Did your aunt leave you anything else? Life insurance?"

I shake my head. "Just a failing bookstore and whatever is in her apartment. I have the place with no lease until the end of the year, but I'm paying the rent and everything."

He seems completely undeterred, nodding again. "All right. So, you need money to replace your phone. Money to do the stuff on this list." He thinks for a second. "Do you want my help, Chloe? If that's not what you want, you need to tell me now to stand down. I'm a lot like my mom in that sense, but at least I know enough to ask before I barge into someone's business."

"What do you have in mind?"

He motions for me to sit. His eyes sparkle and he's got a sexy grin on his face, and since my knees go a little weak at the sight, I have no problem dropping into a chair. "How do you feel about paperwork?" he asks.

CHAPTER 9
FRANCO

"CHLOE, THIS IS JACK MILES."

It's around ten on Tuesday by the time we get through breakfast. I take Chloe over to Easy Start just about the time I know Jack will be taking a break.

He shakes Chloe's hand and lifts his chin at me. "I thought you weren't coming in today, man." He's looking Chloe over and I know his mind is spinning, but he's not saying anything.

Something seems to have shifted in Chloe this morning. She's still wearing her boots and pants that must be two sizes too big, but after spending the night tucked against her ass, I'm actually happy she's hiding what she's got from the world. Under those bulky sweaters, her body is more than what meets the eye. Just like the woman herself.

When I woke this morning with my hand under her

shirt, it was all I could do to keep my fingers from wandering to her breasts, ass, thighs...

"Hi, Jack. Nice to meet you." She shakes his hand, and I can tell Jack's confused, but my buddy's nothing if not cool.

They make small talk about Chloe's aunt Ann and the café, until finally, we get down to business.

"Jack," I say, "since your mom's on temporary hiatus, how would you feel about hiring Chloe for a couple days to get that paperwork sorted?"

Chloe and I talked about the idea in the truck, so I know she's down for it. I don't know if Jack's budget at the shop will allow him to pay Chloe for some very part-time work, but I have a list of ideas a mile long. This is just our first stop.

"Listen," I add, "she needs some capital for some improvements to Ann's place. Won't be a long-term thing, but if you and your pops can find some leeway in the payroll, you can help out Chloe, and I'll bet she can find that purchase order you've been wanting me to deal with."

Jack's thinking it over, but he looks dubious. "I've got to call my dad, Frankie," he says, looking sheepish. "Hiring someone's not that easy. There's taxes and paperwork to consider..."

I hold up a hand to stop him. "Look, I get it. If it's too complicated, no worries. Throwing it out there, that's all."

"Dad's still fishing," Jack reminds me. "But I'll give

him a quick call. If it's a no, you'll know sooner rather than later."

Chloe's face crumples a little, but I give her a reassuring nod. "Come with me," I say, leading her to Carol's desk. "Let's give Jack some privacy while he calls Earl."

She grabs my sleeve as we're walking away. "Franco." Her voice is tiny again, the fading flower starting to droop. "I don't want to cause any trouble…"

"What trouble? This ain't trouble," I assure her. "It's a phone call. Earl will say yes or no, and then we'll go from there." I turn to her and put my hands on her shoulders.

I meant what I said this morning in my kitchen. I don't know why, but I can't stop myself from touching her.

She doesn't seem to mind, so I squeeze gently and lower my voice. "You asking for what you need doesn't inconvenience anybody," I say. "I mean that. Ask. Speak up. Say what you need. If the answer's no…" I shrug one shoulder. "Then fuck it. Shake it off and keep going. Around me, don't ever apologize for asking for what you want."

She is nibbling on her lower lip and watching my face like I have all the answers there. I don't, but what I do know is that the world helps those who help themselves.

If there's anything I can do for her right now, it's to make her realize that.

"Come on." I motion toward Carol's desk.

I show her the stack of paperwork. Shit that hasn't been paid or organized in weeks since Carol stopped coming into the shop every day.

"You'd think that one purchase order wouldn't be that hard to find," I tell her. "But I looked and couldn't find the damn thing."

In the time it takes Jack to call Earl, Chloe digs into the mountain of papers on the desk. She's organized them by date, which...well fuck, I should have thought to do that.

When Jack comes back to the desk, Chloe's got things looking neat enough for someone to sit down and work.

Jack whistles. "Shit, Chloe. You're hired. When can you start?"

Her mouth falls open, and she looks from him to me.

"I'll butt out," I say, nodding. "Let you two talk details."

I wander around the shop, checking what Jack's working on while they chatter, but I keep one eye on Chloe.

She may have been shy and quiet around my family, but she's looking Jack in the eye and laughing, seemingly totally at ease with him. Seeing her connecting with him like that sets a little ember on fire in my gut. It's threatening to turn into a raging jealous inferno when she catches my eye over Jack's shoulder.

She gives me a saucy smirk and draws her lower lip into her mouth.

Something tight and hot uncoils in my chest at that look.

The pouty lips, the light in her eyes. She even tosses a lock of hair over her shoulder, not that I think she does it on purpose. Her body seems lighter, freer, and she's moving around more. It's fucking hot. And now that I know what she's got under those sweaters, I want more of it. More of her.

"Yo." Jack turns suddenly and calls for me, so I join them back at the desk.

Chloe's cheeks are flushed, and she looks happy.

Jack looks relieved.

"Looks like Chloe's going to fit right in," he says. He extends his hand to shake hers again, and I almost interrupt to tell him he already did that and there's no reason to touch her again, but I stop myself and just watch.

She is practically bouncing as I clap my buddy on the shoulder and let him know I'll see him tomorrow.

Chloe follows me back to the truck, but before I can turn over the engine, she reaches across the seats and squeezes my arm. "Thank you," she says, her voice stronger than I think I've heard it. "With what they are paying me, I'll be able to afford even a top-of-the-line, brand-new, all the bells and whistles phone in about a month." She looks down at her hand on my sleeve, and if she's thinking about moving it, she decides against it.

She leaves it there and squeezes. "I may shut down the store for a few weeks while I get things sorted out. We'll see. But Jack said I can make my own hours. I'll find a way to balance it out."

"You'll be able to afford a kick-ass phone in a month?" I repeat. "That's great. That's how long I was planning to extend an interest-free loan for."

She cocks her chin and looks at me. "I'm sorry? What?"

I grin and turn on the engine, then head out toward the mall. "I'm going to buy you a phone today, but it's a loan. Thirty days interest-free. You can start paying me back once you've got some cash flowing."

She starts to complain, but I stop her with a hand. "Chloe, what's the big deal? Are you going to pick the most expensive phone in the place?"

She shakes her head.

"Fine. I'm offering to shell out the cash to get you set up today. It's a safety issue. I won't be able to sleep at night if I think you're going around town without even a way to call the cops. While we're out today, I have a whole list of things to do, remember? So, buckle up and start thinking about what you want in a new phone."

She falls silent again, and I'm sure she's gnawing right through her lower lip.

"Franco," she finally says, breaking through the quiet. "Why? Why are you helping me? I don't think I can do anything to pay you back for all this... I mean, of course I'll pay you back for the phone. Like, no question about it. But giving me a place to stay last night and making me breakfast and now this… It's a lot."

"When I was in my twenties, I was sloppy," I say. "I had a big ego. Big balls. Big head. The whole nine." I laugh and shake my head. "I was a shithead from the word go." I flick a glance at her.

She fully turns in the passenger seat, listening intently as I talk.

"Someone helped me, and now it's my turn to help you. That's what friends do," I explain, but I'm lying to her and myself.

Sure, we're friends…but part of me wants to be so much more. And if I'm being honest, that scares the living shit out me.

CHAPTER 10
CHLOE

AFTER FRANCO TOOK me to get a phone, we stopped by the fire station to talk to one of Vito's buddies who has a business on the side setting up home security systems.

We explain the situation with the store, and the firefighter gives Franco a list of the items they'll need—all of which Franco insists on purchasing himself.

The guy promises to stop by Latterature to install everything after I get wireless internet set up.

"You mind if we make another stop?" he asks. "I'd like to let my sister in on what happened at the café."

I nod, and an immediate feeling of dread clenches my belly. It's nearly dinnertime, and we're headed right back to where everything happened last night.

I don't know what my face looks like, but Franco reaches a hand across the seats and gives my hand a reassuring squeeze.

"You okay?" he asks. "I'll be right there. It's going to be fine."

I look down at his fingers resting lightly on mine. "Yeah," I say. "Of course. I…"

But then I remember. This is not what I want. This is not who I want to be. I'm not going to pretend or lie or make the best of it when what I really feel is scared shitless.

"No," I correct myself. "I'm terrified, honestly. I know it may be childish, and I'll get over it, you know? I will. I'll get over it, through it. It'll get better. But right now, just the thought of going back there makes me feel sick."

He nods, and he laces his fingers through mine rather than pulling his hand away. "I get it," he says. "And it's okay. I don't want to make it worse for you, but I really want to let my sister in on what's going on. I probably should have called her already."

I'm watching our hands and the easy way he holds mine, and I wonder how this is my life.

I'm sure Franco is just *that guy*. He holds hands and flirts with and sleeps with women like it's no big deal. To me, every time he touches me, my body snaps to attention and wants to decode every movement. Every intention. Is he holding my hand to be nice?

I get my answer when he releases my hand quickly and puts both of his hands on the steering wheel as he stares straight ahead.

Right.

He's a good man.

A dutiful son and older brother.

I can be honest with myself about how the man makes me feel, while keeping myself grounded in reality.

This is…friendship, right?

And I need friends, especially here in Star Falls.

We park a few spots away from The Body Shop, and I feel Franco's eyes on me as I stare at my store.

It looks harmless and dark. The handwritten piece of paper I put up inside the door still hangs right where I taped it before we left last night.

I sit motionless as Franco jumps out, comes around, and then opens the passenger door for me.

"Hey," he says, meeting my eyes. "You good?"

I shrug, then nod, then shrug again. "I might need another hug," I mumble, not intending for him to hear.

But he must because he grins, and the sight takes my breath away. His blue eyes flash, and I'm a little embarrassed that he heard me, but hell, this is me trying to be honest. Not hiding.

When we get inside, I'm surprised by the place. I've only been inside one tattoo shop, which is why I've never actually gotten one.

Instead of dingy walls, The Body Shop is decorated in a soothing, cool palette of minimalist, almost midcentury style.

A large gray couch is in the waiting area, covered with pretty pillows that look comfortable and classy. I examine the space in awe, and although I should not be surprised, I am.

"Yo, Echo." Franco drops his keys on the front counter.

The woman behind the counter has hot-pink hair cut short in the front with a sort of curly mullet in back. Her eyes are heavily made-up with dramatic black liner and sharp, glittery pink shadow.

"What's up?" Echo smiles.

"This is Chloe," Franco says, pointing to me.

I take in the chipped black nail polish and torn fishnet top over a ribbed black tank. "So nice to meet you," I say.

"Is Gracie around?" Franco asks.

Echo hooks a thumb toward the back of the shop. "Yeah, your sister's done for the day. She's cleaning up her station. Want me to get her?"

"Please."

Echo heads back through a small door with a peek-aboo window. I can already see they have more security than I do.

While Echo leaves, I notice a mount that would hold a tablet or other small device, which is probably what they use in place of a huge, antique cash register.

"Hey, asshole." Gracie comes bursting through the door, her head cocked and her black locks flying. "What are you doing here on a school night?"

She looks from her brother to me and cocks her head in the other direction, doing a sharp double take. "And hey…Chloe," she says, sounding confused. She comes up to me and kisses my cheek, then crosses her arms over her chest.

"You look beautiful," I tell her sincerely, letting myself point to her arms. "I haven't seen all these yet."

She grins, and I swear there's a blush competing with the rest of the colors on her skin. "Thanks, babe," she says, using the endearment like I'm her oldest friend. "So, what the hell are you two doing here and not at work?" She leaves off the word "together," but I am sure, given the look of amused confusion on her face, she's thinking it.

"So, not great news," Franco says. "Chloe was held up at Latterature last night. Asshole with a knife."

"Oh my God. What? Stop. Are you serious?" Gracie looks at me, but the gravity in her voice and the slight shake I hear there have me nodding soberly.

"Yeah," I say. "It was terrifying. Franco happened to come by to drop off the leftovers I'd forgotten in his truck and nearly stopped the guy. Ran into him leaving my shop."

Gracie shocks me, clasping me in a quick, hard hug, and breathes against my hair. "Are you okay?" she asks. "My God, you weren't hurt, I hope?"

I hug her back and shake my head. "I'm fine, thanks to Franco. He's been taking care of me all day."

She releases me, but only so she can hold my shoulders with both hands and stare into my face. "What the hell? People suck." Gracie finally releases me and throws herself against her brother's chest. "Good on you for being there," she says. "Are you okay?"

He nods and rests his chin on top of her head. "Yeah," he assures her. "Totally fine, just fucking pissed off the guy slipped through my fingers."

She strokes her chin thoughtfully as if putting the pieces together. "That's what the sign on the door means?" she asks. "I went over earlier for coffee and to hang out, but the sign says closed temporarily."

I nod. "I didn't want to give a reason or a timeline," I explain. "I have a lot to figure out before I open the store again."

"That's why we stopped by." Franco is looking at Echo. "Wanted you all to know. This happened yesterday when you were closed here, but whoever did this probably has been casing Main Street. The way I figure it, he noticed a new owner, a young woman by herself. Probably had been inside and saw she had no security and no technology, which means a cash business."

Echo points to a tiny sign on the counter that reads, *We love green but don't accept cash.* "We stopped taking cash like two years ago when Gracie raised the shop minimum."

"Brought in a much more serious clientele," Gracie explains, rolling her eyes. "I can't tell you how many weekends I had to turn away drunk kids with a wad of sweaty twenties wanting to get the cheapest tattoo we could do."

"Not much to steal here," I muse, looking around the shop. I notice a tiny green light up in the corner by the ceiling.

"And we have security," Gracie says. "But not all the stores do. It's too goddamn dark on Main Street around closing." She paces the lobby, a scowl on her face. "You know, just because we have cameras... doesn't mean shit. If there's somebody casing Main Street, we need to amp up security. More lights outside, motion sensors, maybe a security guard. The holidays are coming up, and that means more people, more shoppers, and more opportunities for criminals."

I have a hard time believing the building owner will do anything to improve security, but Gracie has a great point.

I make a note to check my aunt's lease and find out about the building owner and any help they might be willing to provide on the security end of things.

Franco and Gracie are talking about how the criminal got my phone when she looks at me and points right at my chest. "Well, you know you can't go home, right?"

I look from Gracie to Franco and back. "I mean... I..."

Gracie turns to her brother. "She stayed with you last night? Are you going to keep her with you? I'm sure Ma and Pops will put her up. Maybe Bev... Bev has that big house..."

I look between them again, feeling like I'm missing

something. "You don't think I can go home yet?" I ask naïvely. I mean, let's be real. If Franco wants to offer me another night with him, I won't say no. But that's a far cry from me never being able to go back to Aunt Ann's.

"Do you know how easy it will be for that sicko to find you?" Gracie says, true concern marring her features. "Did you use any GPS apps on your phone?"

My stomach sinks. My entire life is in that phone. Over the weeks I've been getting to know Star Falls, I've used my GPS to find everything.

My new place was saved as "home." The shop is saved.

"You have a passcode on your phone?"

"Um," I mumble as my cheeks heat.

I bypassed the feature because I wanted to save time, and I never thought someone would take my phone and use it against me.

Damn it.

"Franco, you can't let her go home alone. Not until they catch the prick who did this or you can beef up the security at her place." Gracie's arms are flailing wildly as she gestures.

Echo is nodding behind the counter. "I agree."

It's dark outside, and the idea of going back home to Aunt Ann's alone is now the only thing I can think about.

I don't want to, but the real reason isn't just fear. One more night in Franco's bed, in Franco's arms, is a gift I would not turn down if it was offered.

"Promise me," Gracie says. She's so intent on him assuring her I'll be safe, I'm sure there's more going on than meets the eye here. Gracie has some story to tell, and while tonight isn't the time, someday I'll ask her.

"We'll deal with it." Franco nods at his sister and Echo, then puts a hand to my elbow. "We got to roll. Just..." He looks at his sister. "Keep your eyes open, Gracie."

She nods somberly and waves at us. "You need anything, Chloe... Wait." But then she stops. "Oh shit. I was going to give you my number."

"I have a phone now. Your brother helped me get a replacement today." If Gracie is surprised by what I tell her, she doesn't show it. She takes my new phone from me and punches in her contact information, then hands the device back to me. "You text me if you need anything," she says, and she's so sincere, I believe she means it.

"Thank you."

"I mean it," she says, giving me another hug. "Anything."

"Thank you," I repeat before she releases me.

Franco and I are quiet once we're back in his truck.

"You know you don't have to—" I start, but he is talking at the same time, so neither one of us hears what the other tried to say.

"Sorry," I laugh. "You first?"

He nods. "My sister makes a good point." He's looking at me with no hint of a smile on his face. "I

149

don't know if it's the best idea for you go to back to your place just yet."

I nod and look down at my hands. I'm clenching my fists in my lap, at war with fear and vulnerability deep inside. I don't know what to say or do.

"Chloe?" Franco's studying my face when I look up at him. "It's going to be okay," he promises.

I nod, but I need a little time with my thoughts. Rather than pretend I'm okay, I say exactly what I'm feeling. "It makes me feel really vulnerable to rely on you the way I need to right now. Can I just think for a minute?"

"Think? About what?" His eyes darken, and he frowns. "Are you thinking about going back home? To Pennsylvania?"

I shrug. I don't know. Maybe this is a sign I should.

"I just need to sort out my feelings," I say. "I'm scared. I'm stressed. I'm overwhelmed. I feel indebted to you for all you've done…" Tears sting my eyes, but I'm not sad. I'm not sure what I am. "It's all just a lot."

He nods and turns the truck on. We sit in front of The Body Shop for a few minutes, the engine idling, the radio off. Just two people together, each lost in thought. Finally, a loud grumble from my stomach breaks the tension.

"Sounds to me like it's dinnertime," Franco says with a grin. "Can I take you someplace? You mind Italian again?"

I think about how much money I have in my account

and desperately wish I could buy him dinner to thank him for all he's done, but before I can protest, he says, "Don't worry. Where we're going, we eat for free."

———

"Your brother really named his restaurant after himself." It's not really a question, more an observation.

Benito's is this cute little place—surprisingly cute. The exterior looks like a house that's been converted into a restaurant. The parking lot is large, and based on how full it is even on a Tuesday night, he must have a successful business.

Franco laughs as he gets out of the truck. "That's my brother."

When we walk inside, I'm immediately greeted by a feeling just like the one I had at his parents' house.

"Franco." The hostess must be close to eighty.

Franco leans down and lets the hostess kiss his cheek. "Rita, this is Chloe. Ann's niece."

The woman turns her hands to me, holding her palms up like she wants to cup my face. I smile at her, unsure whether I should hug her, shake hands, or wait for her to pinch my cheeks. She gasps and shakes her head. "Chloe, well I'll be damned. You're a stunner." She elbows Franco and lifts a brow suggestively. "Keep her away from your brother," she advises.

Franco laughs, and I instinctively slip my hand into the crook of his elbow.

"Rita is Bev's mother," Franco explains.

"Bev is so nice," I say.

A couple comes in behind us, and Rita knows them, so she shoos us past her so she can seat the folks behind us. "It's their anniversary, so they have a reservation. Go have a drink at the bar, and I'll come get you when I have a table for you." Rita greets the couple with her arms outstretched, wishing them an overly loud happy anniversary.

My hand is still at Franco's elbow, but he angles himself so he can rest his hand at the small of my back. "Go ahead," he says.

I weave through the crowd of diners and find only one empty stool at the bar. "I can stand," I say, but Franco's hand is already on the wooden seat as he pulls it out for me.

"What are you drinking?" he asks. "Have whatever you want."

The bartender is insanely hot. Like, I mean she could be a model beautiful.

"Holy smokes," I mumble under my breath. "I think I have a whole new respect for your brother."

Franco lifts a brow and leans closer to hear me.

"If I owned this place, I'd sleep with the bartender too," I say.

Franco's eyelids lower, a seductive, sleepy look like he's picturing me in bed with the gorgeous brunette. "There's more to you than meets the eye, Chloe." His voice is a sensual rasp against my ears, and the hairs on the back of my neck stand at attention.

I'm about to try to say something brilliantly witty when the gorgeous girl behind the bar spots Franco.

"Hey, handsome," she calls over the bar noise. "And who's this? I didn't know you had a girlfriend."

I open my mouth to correct her, but Franco leans over the bar and says, "This is Chloe." He introduces me to the girl whose name is Ashley, and without even taking our order, she sets down two glasses of ice water with a slice of lime on the rim.

She starts pouring alcohol into a shaker and then serves up two candy-apple-red drinks in short glasses. "On me," she says. "Enjoy."

Franco takes one of the drinks and hands the other to me. "You don't have to drink it," he says. "It's a negroni. Pure alcohol. Despite its festive color, it'll get you hammered quick."

Right now, that doesn't sound half bad.

We tap the rims of our glasses together, and I taste a small sip. "That is delicious," I tell him. "And strong."

What's more delicious than the negroni is the feel of Franco's thigh wedged against mine. He's standing beside my stool, his large form shoulder to shoulder with me so the people beside us have some elbow room.

We have hardly sipped our drinks when Benito comes running out front. He's dressed like he's cooking, wearing jeans and a white chef's jacket.

"Yo," he greets his brother with a chin lift and claps

Franco on the back. "Hi, sweetheart," he says to me as though we've known each other for years and not days. "Ma's going to be over the fucking moon," he says, looking from me to Franco. "Her matchmaking has never worked before."

I can't tell if he's teasing or not because Franco smacks his brother on the back and then grabs my drink before motioning for me to follow him. I wave my thanks to Ashley. Her hands are full shaking another round of negronis, but she gives me a chin lift as I hop down off the stool.

Benito seats us himself, doesn't even give us menus. He just asks me if I have any food allergies or things I don't like. I shake my head, and he disappears, promising a meal I'll never forget.

Sassy is our server, and she keeps us going with an endless stream of conversation as she drops off course after course of food. By dessert, I don't think I can eat another bite, so I refuse the cornmeal cake, but Franco has Sassy pack it to go.

"Don't tell my brother I said this," Franco says under his breath, "but that damned cake is my favorite dessert of all time."

I raise my hand and call out, "Benito." But I say it quietly just to tease Franco like I'm going to give his secret away.

He grabs my hand by the wrist, and the moment changes, shifts from something playful to something very different. We swap a look that's both heated and awkward, and he slides his fingers away from my skin. I immediately miss his strength and heat.

Sassy reminds us the meal is on the house.

Franco hands Sassy her tip in cash and thanks her for the meal. Then he stands and kisses her cheek.

She fusses over me, and I realize she doesn't yet know about what happened at the shop—or at least, she isn't bringing it up.

"Am I taking you home with me?" he murmurs, his lips quirked in a smile.

I must be a little tipsy because I say exactly what's on my mind. "Only if you promise I don't have to sleep on the couch," I say.

I am momentarily horrified.

I mean, the man's opened his home to me, and I've just brazenly demanded what…that he sleep with me?

Share his bed?

Spoon me again until I feel his hard length against my bottom?

I feel the flush light up my cheeks, but that's nothing compared to how I feel when he leans down and whispers in my ear.

"Babe, you're not leaving my side tonight," he says with a sly grin, and for a moment…I'm hopeful for more than a hug.

CHAPTER 11
FRANCO

WE WALK through the door of my place together like we're coming home. The feeling is unusual—no, it's more than that. It's fucking weird.

I've had plenty of women back to my place over the years, but never once has the person at my side felt like she belonged there. With me. I'm not sure whether to shake the feeling or embrace it.

I don't have to think long because as soon as we're in the door, we stand side by side taking off our boots. Chloe kicks hers off first and then steps up to me. She's looking me in the face, her sweet lower lip tucked between her teeth.

"Franco, I…"

I have no idea what she's thinking, but she rises on her toes and places a featherlight kiss against my cheek. "Thank you," she whispers, looping her arms around my neck. "For everything today."

I feel like she's moving back, stepping away from me, but I don't want to let her go. I circle my hands around her waist, and that seems to be the invitation she needs to stay right where she is. To come even closer, in fact. "You're...welcome," I manage as she flutters her eyelids shut and sways against me.

I don't know what else to say or how to navigate this. She's going to crash at my place again tonight; I think it's clear we both want that. But what is becoming even clearer is there's more we want from each other than company. More than this chaste thank-you kiss on the cheek.

Do we want more than *that*?

I think so, at least, but I admit I'm not entirely sure. "Are you tipsy?" I ask delicately, not wanting to insult her, but also not wanting to let anything happen when she isn't in a perfectly clear state of mind to make the decision.

Her eyes open, and she releases her hold on my neck. "No," she says.

I hold her tight around the waist. "I'm going to kiss you."

She widens her eyes and licks her lips. Her breath comes in little puffs, nervous and excited. The same as mine. She nods and lifts her face to mine, bringing her nose as close to mine as she can on tiptoe.

I brush my lips against hers, and her sweet, orange-scented breath fills my senses. But just a touch of those plush lips sends my cock into overdrive, and suddenly, my brain is no longer in control.

There is no thinking my way through this. No rational thought that's going to protect me from how complicated I know this is going to get.

For now, though, it's simple.

I want her, and I want her bad.

She tastes divine, and I open my mouth, exploring her depths with my tongue. She mewls against my lips, her hips pressing against my already stiff cock, and I know I'm fucked. Done for. This woman tastes like an angel and is hiding curves that I know were meant to be worshipped. I want to lay her out on my bed and taste every inch of her skin. I want to see her pussy, watch as I touch the trembling flesh. My body is in control now, and I'm just a helpless participant, following the demands of my desire for her.

Her hair is fisted between my fingers and her tits are crushed against my chest. "You want this?" I pant. "It's not too late to say no, and I'll take a cold shower and sleep on the—"

I can't even get the offer out before she's rasping, "I want this. I want you. If you want me, then God, Franco…please…"

While it's nowhere near as picture-perfect as it is in the movies, we kiss and grope and strip out of our clothes the entire stumbling walk up the stairs to my bedroom.

By the time we make it to the bed, Chloe's sweater

is gone, and she's fumbling with the button on her cargo pants. I stop her with a hand.

"That's my job," I growl, looking pointedly at her body. "I'm going to take such good care of you."

I can see her entire body tremble under my gaze. Her nipples are so hard I can see the thick peaks just begging to be nibbled through the cups of her bra. She stands with her hands at her sides, looking like she has absolutely no idea what to do.

I shuck off my jeans and socks but leave on my boxer briefs. If I expose my cock just yet, that'll be it. Once my skin touches hers, there'll be no going back. And I want to take my time with this.

She stands there wide-eyed, her lips parted, those erect buds practically shredding through her bra. I close the space between us and lift her chin so our eyes meet, and I just look at her.

"You're beautiful, Chloe," I say, picking up a lock of her hair between two fingers. "And I want to see every inch of you."

She shivers, harder this time, but her eyes never leave mine. "You're unbelievable," she whispers. "Not like I don't believe you. I mean like, you're so gorgeous."

"Thank you, baby." I'm glad she likes what she sees, but right now, all I care about is how hungry I am for her.

I start with the button on her pants, unfastening it

easily. Then I work the zipper down and urge the waist-band away from her hips.

Chloe's got some curves to her, and I got just a taste of her last night when my dick cuddled up her ass like it was magnetically attracted.

She's wearing boy short-type underwear today, and I shove those down, exposing her trimmed mound. She gasps, a thrilling sound that's heavy with wanting. She clutches my bare shoulders as she steps out of the panties. I toss them aside and look at her. Her hair spills over her shoulders as her cheeks flush. I'm so goddamn hard, I want to get myself off fast so I can savor the experience and get hard again.

But no. I'm not going to blow in ten seconds like a kid. I'm going to take my sweet time, no matter how my dick protests.

She shivers and crosses her arms lightly over her chest.

I shove aside the blankets, and she dives into my bed headfirst, making me laugh. "There's so much more to you than meets the eye," I tell her. "You're serious and quiet, but you're not. You're funny and snarky and playful."

"I'm also really, really turned on," she adds.

I laugh again and climb in bed beside her. I tug the covers over her legs to warm her feet and lie on my side next to her. My raging hard-on knocks into the outside of her thigh as I tuck in closer. "Lie still."

She nods and lies on her back. Waiting. I haven't

removed her bra yet, but I really want to take my time getting there.

I support my weight on one arm, so my other hand is free to stroke her collarbone and neck. I kiss her throat and her sternum, warming her body with my breath and heat until she squirms under my touch, and I know she's wanting more.

I trail my fingertips along the top of her bra cup, pressing lightly over the tip of her nipple that's desperately trying to break its way through the fabric to get to me. I pinch her softly, watching for her body's pleasure tell. She gasps and her legs quiver at the gentle pressure, so I try again, harder this time.

"Oh God," she pants.

Fuck. I haven't even touched her yet, and she's crying out to heaven? Chloe is going to be more fun than I've had in a long time.

I ease the cup away from one of her breasts, pushing the fabric down so her nipple peeks out. The rosy tip is dark, hard, and thick, and just seeing it makes me want to bite down and suck deep, but I start slow, licking and flicking the tender skin with the tip of my tongue. She weaves her fingers through my hair and presses my head closer, but I want to take my time. Watch her passion ratchet up until she's explosive.

I lift my head away from her breast and she whimpers in displeasure, but she's quickly changing her tune as I lock my mouth on to that rosy bud and suck it deep into my mouth.

Her hips jerk and her hands are back in my hair as I work my tongue in leisurely circles around the dark areola, stopping only to nip the erect tip between my teeth and suck it long and hard into my mouth.

Her legs are quivering by the time I get to the other breast. I climb over her body, but instead of coming to rest on her other side, I anchor my weight above her as I straddle her hips. I grind lightly against her, and she rolls her eyes back in her head and slams her lids shut.

Her breasts are full, and I cup one in my hand, feeding her nipple into my mouth. I suck this side harder, leaving a wet mark and a faint pink color when I lift my mouth to check on her.

"This good?" I ask.

She slams her eyes open and grips the blankets between tight fingers. "Don't you dare freaking stop."

I laugh and leave her perfect nipples pointing at the ceiling, her bra cups shoved down near the band, as I move to the foot of the bed. I kneel beside her and run my fingers up and down her thighs, kneading the muscles until her mouth falls open and little purrs of pleasure escape from between her lips.

I gently open her legs. "I want to look at you," I say, warning her. I spread her knees wide and settle between her legs. I can see the tiny hairs on her thighs are pebbled and her fingers are still clenched tight, but she looks blissed out. With her nipples exposed and erect, I could sink myself deep and blow my wad in seconds, but I'm not sure I'm even going to fuck her. I'm having way too much fun exploring.

I palm both of her thighs on my way higher, then I scoot closer between her legs so I can see her pussy. With one hand, I smooth the trimmed hair, getting her used to my touch. She sighs until I take two fingers and stroke her drenched seam. She bucks against the mattress lightly, but I use my other hand on her belly to still her.

When I brush the right spot, she jerks and releases a moan that sends a bolt of electricity to my cock. I'm dripping at the tip now, my cock so fucking hard it's difficult to get comfortable on my belly, but I'm too focused on discovering all her buttons to stop. Her legs open even wider, and I encourage her.

"That's it," I say, the scent of her arousal making my mouth water.

I work my thumb in gentle circles, watching how she writhes beneath me, her thighs tense, her breathing ragged, and I work my fingers inside little by little. She's grinding her hips so hard, trying to draw me deeper inside, that she's practically slamming her body down on my fingers. But I want to be the one to bring her pleasure. I want to control when she comes, how hard, how long, so I can watch her fall apart and come back together.

"Open your legs wider," I tell her.

I don't move my hand from her pussy, but I use the other hand to lift the knee closest to me a little higher.

She follows my lead, bending her knees so her feet are on the mattress and then letting her legs fall open.

I lower my face to her inner thigh and lick and kiss her while I stroke her clit with increasingly firm pressure. My fingers are soaked but nowhere near fully inside her yet, and she's jerking her hips rhythmically like she's chasing her own private high.

When I know she's close to spilling over the edge, I slide my fingers deep inside her and piston my arm so I can move in and out without ever fully taking my fingers from her body. My fingers are all the way inside, while my thumb works her clit, and together, my hand cups her sex and strokes and fucks her. I take my time, the only rush the one I'll get when I finally make her scream.

"Oh fuck, Franco."

She's off then, riding the wave, lost to the pleasure my fingers and mouth brought her. I can feel every spasm of her climax against my fingers and in my hair because she's grabbed my head with both hands as she thrashes beneath me.

She slows quietly and comes to a panting rest just as I gently pull my fingers from her pussy. She struggles to open her eyes, but she does, and I stare at her as I slide one finger and then the other into my mouth.

"I want to taste *you*," she says, quiet determination in her voice.

"I'm all yours. Do with me as you please."

I hold her in my arms for what seems like a second

before she's up on her knees. She unclasps her bra and tosses it aside. My boxer briefs are off and chasing her bra into a corner of my room while she leans back on her heels.

"Franco," she says quietly, her voice fragile.

"Yeah?"

She swallows hard. "I mean... Everything I want to do with you... It's overwhelming. I want to ride you. I want to suck you. You're so freaking beautiful and sexy, and we hardly even know each other. Is this stupid fast? Or just like two people scratching an itch?"

I shrug one shoulder.

The words die in my throat as I feel her lips close over my shaft. And I'm suddenly not soft anymore.

CHAPTER 12
CHLOE

TWO WEEKS *Later*

Franco is snoring lightly behind me. His body is entangled with mine. One arm is thrown over my naked torso, and our calves and thighs are knitted together in a leg-lock.

This feels so normal. So right.

Being with him like this is like nothing I've ever experienced. He feels like my person now. This feels like falling in love.

Every morning, I wake up convinced that last night was the *last* night. But mornings keep turning into nights, day after day, and here I am. Still sleeping in his bed. Still naked. And yet still feeling the pressure of time passing.

My tummy flips over, knowing it's time for this

fairy tale to come to an end. I have to return to my apartment, pay my rent, and go back to my own life.

I slide out from underneath him, carefully moving his limbs off me so I don't wake him. I need coffee. I need to spend some time thinking about the future. For us. For me. For the bookstore…for everything.

I sigh deeply as I'm making us coffee.

"What's wrong?" he asks, walking into the kitchen as he scratches at his chest.

"Nothing."

He raises an eyebrow as his eyes rake over me. "Nothing?" he repeats, sliding an arm around my middle to pull me into a hug. "That sigh means something."

I shrug a shoulder, not wanting to talk about the mix of emotions I'm feeling. I've already overstayed my welcome. One night turned into two, which then turned into a week, and here we are—two weeks later.

"Dinner at my parents' tomorrow?" he asks. The question is casual, but his voice is not.

My heart catches in my chest, and I measure the grounds carefully because there is a slight shake in my hand. "I'd love to go," I say. "But that would be the fourth weekend in a row. The first time your parents invited me and then the last two you brought me with you. Don't you think your family might start to get ideas about…"

I trail off because there is no us. I mean, of course there isn't. But now could be the right time to ask.

"What do you think?" I click on the coffee to brew and join him at the table.

"I think my ma is onto us. She suspects at least." He rubs his forehead just as there's a knock at the door. A loud one. "Fuck," he mutters.

I'm dressed in one of Franco's tank tops, no bra, and wearing just my underwear on the bottom. He's shirtless and in his pajama pants.

"There's only one person who pops by at this hour. You think my ma's going to believe we just had a sleepover?"

I frantically look toward the door. If he didn't seem so unnerved by this, I wouldn't be either. But he's giving off very strong vibes.

He's most definitely not ready for there to be an "us."

I leap up and reassure him. "I'll go get dressed."

Before he says anything, I bound upstairs. I hear the door unlock, and Lucia's voice carries through the house.

"Ma, I already told you. I'm renting. I don't even know if the landlord would allow it."

I quickly make Franco's bed and scan the bedroom for any signs of sex. A wave of deep sadness fills my chest as I realize what I'm up here doing. I'm hiding.

I gather all my things from the bathroom and pack up my bags. I fold the extra blankets and pillows and stack everything.

Then, I wait.

Lucia has to know I'm here.

My car is parked in Franco's driveway.

Damn.

I'm all packed up and sitting on the edge of Franco's bed when he plods upstairs. He notices me just sitting there and cocks his chin.

"What's going on?" he asks, looking around the room, until his eyes land on my bags.

I give him a stiff smile. "I need to get back to my aunt's. The rent is due today. I've spent plenty of time squatting at your place. It's time we get back to normal."

The fairy tale has gone on far too long. Longer than I should've allowed it, because now, I'm afraid my heart can't handle life without him in it.

He scrubs a hand over his chin and nods. "Whatever you want, babe." He looks like he wants to say more, but he just asks, "Are you planning on coming to dinner tomorrow night?"

I stand and shake my head slowly. "You've all hosted me for long enough. I should get back to my place, restock the fridge, and clean. There has to be a thick layer of dust by now."

"What's that mean?"

"It's dirty."

He shakes his head. "About the hosting?"

I glance down at my feet, feeling more uneasy and sadder than I thought possible. "I'm going to skip a week. Let you guys have a family meal without me."

He smiles, but the light doesn't reach his eyes. His lips are tight, and he's got a fist clenched over his chest. "Whatever you want, Chloe. Will I see you at the install tomorrow? Vito and his buddies were planning on being at your shop around eight."

I nod. "Absolutely. And you'll see me at Easy Start on Monday."

This feels absolutely horrific. Way worse than what I'd imagined. He's not asking me to stay. He's not asking to see me again. He's not saying much of anything.

It was just sex, Chloe, I remind myself. Franco is gorgeous and probably has lots of flings like this.

We hardly know each other. I have to remind myself that this didn't mean to him what it did to me. Just because I've been more real and more open doesn't mean that what's happening in my heart is happening in his.

My legs feel weak, but I stand and give Franco my most sincere smile. "Thank you so, so much for all you've done." I laugh and there are tears behind it, so I can't let it go on too long. "You're..." I trail off because I can't finish without crying.

He knows what he is. I'm the one who doesn't know what she is. Not anymore. He only helped me see a side of myself that I want to develop. And for that, I am truly thankful.

I want to touch him, throw myself against that bare chest and thank him, but I know if I smell him again, the

173

musk and cologne of his skin against mine, I will start sobbing. So I don't. I grab my things in a rush and try to brighten my voice to cover the quivering.

"So, this was fun," I say a little too maniacally as I grab my bags.

I lug my things down the stairs, and Franco stays at the top, just watching me.

"Five-star review. Would highly recommend."

The coffee I made is untouched in the kitchen, which I notice as I'm frantically scouring the counter for my keys.

"Don't forget to turn off the coffee!" I yell, reminding him because his memory is shit when it comes to things like appliances. "Will you be there tomorrow?" I ask. "At the shop." But then I realize that sounds like I'm asking him to see me again, and I don't want to pin him down. Don't want to assume. "No worries either way."

I find my keys, and with Franco still at the top of the stairs looking down, I slide into my boots. "See you soon," I call out awkwardly, hustling out the front door.

And that's all the goodbye I can manage. I tug the door closed behind me, throw my stuff in my trunk, and get into my car. And by some miracle, I am able to keep the tears from flowing until I pull away.

CHAPTER 13
FRANCO

I KNEW LETTING her go would be a mistake.

But I did nothing to stop her because I'm an idiot and somehow convinced myself she needed space.

I've parked my truck outside Latterature, but it's early. Way too early. It looks like I'm here before Chloe, and anxiety spikes through my chest. I'm worried, first and foremost, because after she left in such a rush yesterday, I didn't hear from her. Not a call, not a text. Not a damn word.

I rake a hand through my hair and check my phone for the millionth time. I hardly slept a wink last night, wondering if she'd made it home safe. If her place was okay. If she was able to sleep. If she missed being with me.

We'd talked plenty about her going back to Ann's to pay the rent in the days before it was due. What we never talked about was what it all meant. What we'd do after she bought herself another month in Ann's place.

Ann's place. Yeah, I say that because it doesn't feel right calling it Chloe's place. The last couple weeks, I've been acting as though Chloe's place is with me.

But is it?

I've got to admit, something in me panicked and shut down hard when my ma showed up yesterday.

She absolutely knows I've been with Chloe. There's no way she *can't* know. And although we've kept things cool around my family, bringing Chloe to two family dinners… That was a first. A first that I assured myself was fine, didn't mean anything. But when Ma showed up, acting like she did, I started freaking out. And my level of freak-out boiled over like a pot filled to the top with water when Ma told me why she'd dropped in yesterday.

As usual, I hadn't been answering my phone—because *sex*—so Ma stopped by my place yesterday to see *Chloe*, not me.

I see the lights go on in the shop, so I get out of the truck and jog up to the store. I knock lightly on the door. I see soft shadows under Chloe's eyes when she looks up at me. She looks like she got as little sleep as I did, but she smiles at me as she unlocks the door and lets me in.

"Hey," I say softly, wanting nothing more than to touch her.

Her face falls completely as she peers over my shoulder.

"Hey, asshole." Vito claps me on the back as he walks up behind me. "Chloe." His voice is so sweet when he says her name. "This is Evan."

She smiles at them both, her eyes never meeting mine. "You're right on time. Thanks for coming," Chloe replies as they get closer.

Right away, Evan gives Chloe a look that makes me want to tear the eyes from his head.

Breathe, Franco.

Chloe asks Evan if they need her for anything because she'd like to go into the kitchen and make us all coffee and some breakfast. She writes down the Wi-Fi password and network name she'd like to use, and my brother gets to work setting up her new router.

Within a few hours, she'll have wireless internet for the store, a tablet for ringing up customers, and a basic security system.

She'll be all set.

She won't need me.

Not anymore.

I wander the stacks while Evan and Vito look at the wiring and drill mounts for the camera heads into the walls and ceiling. Honestly, I don't even know why I'm here. I'm useless at electronic shit.

And other than supervising to make sure my shit-head brother and his friend do what, technically, I'm paying them to do, there's no point in me being here.

179

It's Sunday, and we're all going to Ma's for dinner in a couple hours. I may as well go home, go for a run. Go work out in the garage. I could go anywhere, but here is the only place I want to be.

I pull a book from the shelves and drop into one of the old chairs to skim through it. The words swim in front of my eyes. All I can think about is Chloe. I hear her voice as she chats with Vito and Evan, answering their questions. I'm lost in thought when I feel her hand on my shoulder.

"I made you a coffee." She is smiling at me, no judgment in her voice at all, but the sadness on her face makes me sure she's as confused or hurting as I am.

"Are you charging those assholes for their drinks?" I take the coffee from her with a grin. "No freebies. Not even for family."

She looks a little confused by that, and I realize it was the wrong thing to say. Maybe she thinks I'm suggesting she and I are family? I've got to get my fucking boot dislodged from my mouth before I say something that can't be taken back.

"Shush. I'd better see if Vito and Evan need me," she says softly.

"Wait." I stand and put a hand on her arm. She turns to me, and I set the cup of coffee on the chair. "I've been telling you not to hide from me, and I've been hiding from you. No, maybe from myself." I scrub a hand through my hair and shake my head. "I never should have let you leave yesterday without talking."

"Yo." My brother's voice echoes through the store, and I wince. He's calling out to Evan to hold the ladder, and I realize this is not the time or the place to have this talk.

"Can I see you?" I ask. "We need to talk."

She nods. "Why don't you come to my place after dinner? Or you can call me."

I feel like the tiny voice she's using means she's afraid I'm going to let her down, break her heart. That maybe the phone option was a way to let me off easy— or maybe make it easier on her.

"No phone," I say. "I want to look you in the eye and be real with you. Even if it's not easy. Can we do that?"

She nods again, and a wave of absolute pain washes over me. I don't want sad Chloe. I don't want her braced for the bad news that isn't going to come. I want the spunky, awkward, sweet woman who demanded hugs from my self-serve comfort bar. Maybe she's become the comfort bar for me now.

"Can I kiss you?" I ask. "A hug, anything? I don't like how we left things. I want to make it right."

She parts her lips and grins. "Are you trying to proposition me in my own store? My aunt will turn over in her grave."

"This isn't about sex," I growl and tug her to my chest. I hold her against me and breathe in her hair. She smells different today, like a vanilla candle with something tropical, maybe pineapple. I don't care if she smells like the city dump after a fire. Once my arms are around her, I'm sure I never want to let her go.

"Latterature's got a kick-ass security system—bam!" Vito pounds against the dinner table, making the plates and flatware clank.

"For fuck's sake, V." Benny nearly spills the glass of red wine he was pouring and shoots our brother a dark look.

Ma and Pops glare at Vito, but then my ma nods. "I'm glad. That robbery…" She shakes her head and shivers, then makes the sign of the cross over her forehead and heart. "I've got a daughter who works on that street and a future daughter-in-law, God willing, to be concerned about."

When she says future daughter-in-law, all eyes at the table fly to me.

"Oooooh," Benito teases. "Did Ma's matchmaking finally work on you, Franco? I call dibs on best man."

Vito's about to start his bullshit when Gracie speaks up. "She's talking about me, you dumb fuck. Chloe and I are very happy together, thank you very much."

Pops holds both hands as if surrendering. "I love my children whether they are gay, straight, or whatever."

All four of us kids look at my dad with expressions that range from shock to amusement. He shoves his reading glasses onto his hair and shrugs.

"What's whatever?" Ma asks, looking incredibly concerned, like she's ready to run out and make sure whoever this person is, they are happy and content in their life. That's one thing I can say about Mario and Lucia. They are unwaveringly supportive. When Vito wanted to marry a stripper, all they cared about was if he was happy.

My dad lifts his silver brows and shrugs. "Whatever they want to be, as long as they're happy."

I polish off my pasta and salad as they start to bicker about happiness, then get up to clear my plate. I'm in the kitchen rinsing my dish under the faucet when I feel a hand at my back.

"Son." Ma stands behind me, her eyes worried and her lips drawn. "You've been very quiet tonight. And I notice Chloe didn't join us for family dinner. I've been almost sick all evening thinking I did something to come between you two. I shouldn't have shown up the way I did today. I'm sorry, baby. I…"

I turn and face my mom, but all the fire has gone out of my frustration and anger at her meddling. Now I'm just curious.

"When you first tried to set me up with Chloe…" I say, leaning my ass against the sink. "Why? Why her, Ma? Is she just someone who was there?"

My mom is quiet for a minute. She's wearing a new color lipstick today, which is unusual. I make a note to ask her about it. It's a softer color, and I don't remember her ever wearing light colors. Ma's usually bold and dramatic in everything she does, from nails to hair to lips.

"You know Ann and I were very close," she says, and I nod. "And I don't know how to explain it. I just had a feeling, Franco. When I first met Chloe, I knew she was supposed to be part of our family. I never considered anything but introducing her to you. Not Benny or Vito. I just thought she would be perfect for you. It was like I could see it, and I never questioned it. But I'm sorry if I came on too strong or brought you any trouble."

Ma looks genuinely apologetic, but none of this is really her fault. That falls squarely on me.

"You're a buttinski, and I love you." I lean down to kiss my mother's cheek. "What's up with the lipstick? It's different, but I like it."

She scowls and raises one of those brows at me dramatically. She shakes her head as she sighs. "Carol. That woman. I wish she'd just get over things with Earl and at least go back to work at Easy Start. She's doing everything she can to make some money for herself, including selling this makeup now. She did makeovers on all us girls." Ma cups her belly as she laughs. "Wait till you see Sassy. Carol tried to get all of us to do this dewy, natural look the kids are doing. We all looked like we were sweating. And these stripes on the nose the girls are doing now?" Ma takes two fingers and pretends to draw lines on either side of her nose. "Have you seen that? Like I want to change the shape of this schnoz at my age? What's a little brown stuff gonna do? Anybody within a mile would see me and this thing coming. Why would I spend an hour dab-dab-dabbing all around my nose?"

I laugh. "I think that's called contouring, Ma."

"Contour, schmontour. I bought some of the crap she's selling just to support her, but this—" she points to her lips "—this tiger won't be changing the color of her stripes for very long."

We laugh, but then I grow serious. "So, are you saying you think Carol should get back with Earl? I thought she was off on some new path with Ray?"

"Well, I was talking about her job, specifically," my mom says. "I have opinions about the situation with Earl."

I cross my arms over my chest, bracing myself for Ma's opinions, but she suddenly goes silent. "Ma?" I urge, lifting my brows at her. "You said you have opinions?"

"Son, you know how I feel about divorce."

"Necessary evil." I'm well aware of the fact that Ma takes her wedding vows seriously, and that she feels others should as well. But when the circumstances are harmful, she's fully in support of people doing what they need to be safe. Happiness, though, is another story.

She nods. "I've started to consider other perspectives," she says. "You know I love Earl. He's a good man, and he loves Carol and Jack. Has always been a good provider. As far as I know, and I think I would know—Carol doesn't have a private bone in her body— he's never been unfaithful."

I nod, wondering where this is going. I know Earl is a good man and my mother is a good woman. If she's changing her perspective on marriage, I'm curious to see how. And even more curious to know why.

She looks at me with a strange twist to her lips and a scowl in her brow.

"Ma?" I press. "What is it?"

She looks like she's debating whether or not to say anything, but then she blurts it all out in a rush. "Earl doesn't satisfy Carol sexually. Like, not at all. I don't think she's ever, in all their years of marriage, had an orgasm with him."

"Sweet baby Jesus," I groan. "Ma, the man's my boss. I don't need to know—"

"You asked," she snaps. "And Ray Morris, God bless his little—well, I guess it's not so little, to hear Carol talk."

"Ma, I love you, but can we fast-forward to the point?"

She smiles and shakes her head. "I've been pretty rigid in my beliefs most of my life. But I never had a reason to see things differently. Marriage is forever, and unless someone's drinking or violent or something else…"

Hearing that makes me think of what Chloe told me about her parents. Her father was both, and yet her mother stayed. And it cost her mother close ties with her family.

"When Carol first left Earl, I thought she was being foolish. I called her selfish. To her face." Ma's voice cracks a bit on that admission. "But then Carol opened up. Broke down. You know she had that precancerous polyp removed last year, and…"

I almost tune out because if there is one thing I don't want to hear about right after dinner, it's my mother's friends' polyp stories. "Ma."

"All right, all right, just you wait. You get to my age, and everybody's got stuff, son. Anyway, she realized that if she died, she'd have spent her whole life married to a good man. And there's not a thing in the world wrong with that. But Carol said she wanted a great love. Before it was too late to find it." She blots a tear from her eye with the back of her hand. "And I don't know if she'll have some great romance with Ray, but who the heck am I to judge? I've had it all with your father."

She reaches out and touches my arm. "Anyway, are you all right, son? I shouldn't have just popped over this morning either. It wasn't right of me."

"I'm great," I tell her. "Ma, I wouldn't change anything about you. I want you in my life. Although, maybe in the future, give me a few hours to reply before you show up." I hold her close and tight, pressing down her helmet of hair with a loud kiss. "I love you, Ma. You have nothing to apologize for."

I'm heading out of the kitchen when Ma calls after me.

"Yeah?" I turn back to see Ma standing at the sink looking concerned. "I think Chloe should have Mama Dog. I talked to Bev about letting her adopt if she can get the okay from Ann's landlord. I know she doesn't have a yard at that place, but I'd feel a lot better if she had a security system or a good, strong dog with her in that apartment."

I'm not sure why Ma's telling me this, but I nod. "Sounds like a good suggestion. You should tell her," I say, but I'm not being shitty about it. No matter what happens between Chloe and me, my family has to develop their own relationships with her. Without lodging my ass right between them.

Ma nods as if she understands. Maybe Ma will tone down her meddling a bit, but I wouldn't want her to completely walk away from us kids. Balance. It looks like my mom is actively practicing balance. "I'll give her a call this week," she says. "I was hoping she'd come to dinner tonight, but…" She looks like she's about to launch into a lecture or an apology, so I give her a smile.

"Ma, it's all good. I've got to run."

She nods, a smile on her face, and I stop at the table to give my dad and siblings goodbye kisses. Benny already left without saying goodbye or clearing his plate, I notice, and Vito and Gracie are arguing about something, while my pops shakes his head.

"You want to take one or two of these idiots with you?" Pops asks good-naturedly.

I kiss him goodbye and head out before anyone can drag me into a fight or send me off with leftovers. I've got someplace I want to be.

CHAPTER 14
CHLOE

A KNOCK at the door wakes me from a deep sleep. I squint and check my phone.

Damn.

Three missed texts from Franco.

"I'm coming!" I shout, clearing the sleep from my eyes.

I barely slept a wink my first night back here at Aunt Ann's. I was so terrified of being here alone. Not to mention heartsick at being *anyplace* without Franco.

I doubt I slept for two hours last night. After the excitement of getting the security system installed at my shop, I came back here, changed into something comfy, sat down on my couch to read, and wham.

I check the peephole and see Franco's worried stare through the fisheye.

I quickly open the door to let him in and ignore the butterflies in my stomach.

"Hi," I say. "I'm sorry I missed your texts. I fell asleep on the couch and slept like the dead."

He looks me over, from my sleep-messed hair to what I'm wearing. His emotions are all over his face—concern, relief, and then amusement.

"I'm just glad you're okay," he says. "I mean, you are okay, right?"

I nod. "Come on in." I'm wearing only shorts and a loose tank top, so the last thing I need is to give the neighbors a show.

He comes in, and I lock the door. "Did you want anything to drink?" I ask. "I'm going to go change."

He grabs my arm and tugs me close. "Don't change," he says, his voice low.

"You like my tank?" I tease. It's one of his. I didn't mean to steal it, but in my rush to gather up my clothes, one of his tanks—no doubt discarded hastily while we were stripping off our clothes—got tangled up with mine. "I was planning to return it. I accidentally packed it, and…well, it smells like you."

If he's not catching the vibe I'm throwing, then I know we're over. I can't be any more obvious without coming out and saying exactly how I feel.

At my admission, he lowers his chin to the top of my head and holds me against his chest. He breathes deeply. "How is it possible to miss someone so much? I just saw you this morning."

Yes.

Everything inside me starts to tingle in excitement.

I wrap my arms around his waist and close my eyes. I can smell the garlic and tomato lingering in his clothes from dinner with his parents. But deeper, on my second intake of air, it's all him.

My legs go weak, and we just hold each other, arms tight, no words needed between us.

I'm the one who finally breaks the hug. In just a thin tank and paper-thin shorts, my body is throwing a fit that all I'm doing is hugging this man.

But he's here to talk.

I need to eliminate my distracted libido from this conversation.

I lace my fingers through his, and we sit on my aunt's couch side by side. Then I grab the crocheted afghan I was sleeping under, my favorite of hers, a soft dusty-pink shell pattern, and cover myself up to my chin.

"No distractions," I explain. "I want to be focused on our talk."

He laughs, and we each scoot to separate ends of the couch. We put our feet together on the middle cushion so at least our legs are close.

"Ma tells me you might want Mama Dog," I say. "Is that your idea or hers?"

Oh God. He starts right in on it, doesn't he? "Well," I say. I nibble my lower lip and try to think how to say this without really saying it. But then I figure, nope. Honesty. For better or worse, I'm putting my truth out there. "I do want the dog. I know it's crazy, but I sort of hoped if there was something here—" I wave between him and me "—that I could use your yard for her sometimes. I mean, that's if I can get the landlord to approve her here."

Even as I say the words, I know they aren't entirely true, so I walk it back.

"God, that's not it either. Not really." I look the man on my couch in the face and decide for real this time, I'm putting myself out there. "Franco, I…" I look down at my hands. "I know it's fast," I say, "but I'm falling for you. And I… I… I'm…I'm gonna shut up now. I think I've said enough."

Chickenshit.

I'm rambling like an absolute teenager, but God, if that's not what this feels like. I bite my lip to stop myself from professing all my needs.

He quietly gets up from the couch. He doesn't say anything. He just paces and clenches his hands into fists. Paces and clenches.

I rush on to fill the silence between us. "I get it, Franco. You're not in the same place as me. And like I said, it's all happening so, so fast. You've done a lot for me the last couple of weeks, and I have been so happy. Really happy. With you. You gave me a reason to stay in Star Falls, you know? But if you don't feel the same, I understand. It's okay. Maybe this isn't where I'm supposed to be after all."

He stops pacing and looks at me. "You can't make that decision because of me, Chloe." His voice is low.

"You need to choose the life you want for yourself. Whether or not I'm in it, I don't want you to stay and run your aunt's business if that's not really what you want. And if you're not sure…"

"What do you want?" I ask, tucking the blanket tighter around my body. This is a hard conversation to have without any real clothes on. "Like, really want, Franco? We haven't talked much about your past dating life or if you want to settle down with someone. Have a family…" I swallow against the sudden dryness in my mouth. "You can have anything you want," I remind him.

Please say me. Please.

He sighs and rubs his fingers along his forehead. The hair has flopped down out of its perfect style, and he looks torn. "It's not… It's not that…" He starts pacing again.

I get up off the couch.

Tonight is about our words.

Our heads.

Our hearts.

"I'm falling in love with you," I say simply. "I'm sure of it. I've never felt this way about anyone before. And I know it's too fast. Maybe to you it was an easy fling. Something that was fun while you were helping me out. And that's okay. I'll be okay." I put a hand on his sleeve, trying hard to keep my touch light. As much as I want to be brave, to be strong, standing here in underwear and his tank top pouring out my feelings feels horribly vulnerable. Horribly exposed.

But I think about who I want to be. The life I want to have. I'm not sure if Star Falls is going to be home for me. I'm not sure that I want my aunt's store and apartment and her things. I want my own life. Not a hand-me-down. Franco is the very first thing I've ever chosen for myself. Asked for. I have to be okay if he doesn't want me too. I just have to be.

Franco swallows, and I watch the knob in his throat move. His plush lips, so kissable and soft and full, pinch together. He's still not talking. Still not opening up to me.

That's answer enough for me. I don't just want to own my own truth. I want to be worthy of his.

"Were your parents ever happy?" he asks. He sounds young. Almost meek.

I shake my head. "Not that I ever knew or saw. I mean, I suppose when they were young, right? They had to be for a time. Why?"

He stalks back to the couch and takes his place at the far end. "I've never known anyone like my parents. Anyone who got a happily ever after."

I nod. I understand that. "I want that," I tell him. "But it only works when both people want it and work toward it together."

"What if we don't?" he asks. "What if someday you wake up and think, fuck, why this guy? I want a guy who reads. A guy who knows all the book stuff I love so much. That's never going to be me, Chloe. I read, yeah, but your life is a bookstore. Someday you might think I'm fucking stupid. Beneath you."

I shrug. "I don't know why that would happen. I don't think that now. And as far as I can tell, most of the time, the truth is something we either embrace or ignore. Unless it's hidden from us so we can't really face it. You've been open about what you read, and that hasn't changed how I feel about you. So, if you're not hiding anything and I'm not ignoring what you really are…"

He nods, but he looks unsettled. He's fidgeting on the couch, so I sit up and let the blanket of armor fall away again.

"Tell me," I say gently. "Are you afraid of the future and what might change? Or are you not sure what you feel right now?"

"I know exactly what I feel, and I…" His eyes shimmer, becoming even more intense. "I don't understand it. A month ago, my life was perfect. I had everything I could want. I had my shit together. But then you and those shitkicker boots come to Star Falls, and all of a sudden, everything changes."

"Changes how?" I ask. "I mean, staying with you was a lot. I get that. And I'm sorry."

His expression darkens. "I'm sorry about yesterday, babe. I was freaked out." He shakes his head and sighs, letting out a huge chest full of tension. I can see his shoulders lower. "My mother came to my place looking for you. She thought you'd already moved in and wanted to offer to help you clear out Ann's things."

"She did?" No wonder the poor guy freaked out.

We haven't even had five minutes to talk about what this is, let alone have it on family blast.

He nods. "I'm sorry, though. I shouldn't have let you leave like that. I shouldn't have let you spend the night here last night without even checking in on you. I couldn't even send a fucking text."

"I'm a grown woman, Franco. If anything was wrong, I have options now. A phone. Gas in my car. And the numbers of everyone in your family." I chuckle at that. "I might have ended up on Lucia's couch, but I wouldn't have been alone or in danger."

"I don't want you calling them when you need something," he growls. "I want to be the one you go to. Wake up to. Sleep with. I mean, next to…as well as the other stuff."

We both smile, and the air between us crackles with possibility.

"It's been two weeks, and it's like I don't even know myself anymore," he says, his voice faraway. "But the weird part is, I've never felt more like myself. You make my life feel whole. What did I have before? It's like I was just killing time. Waiting for you."

My mouth falls open because I'm not sure I heard him right. "Really?"

He nods. "Yes, really. I haven't laughed, worried, or had fun in an entire relationship with someone else like

I have with you these past two weeks. It's terrifying. Like, what the hell was I doing before?"

"Practicing?" I offer. "Probably mostly practicing sex. You're really good at it now, though. Good enough I think you only need to do it with me from now on."

He laughs. "Two weeks, man, that's nothing. The blink of an eye."

"It is something," I correct him. "It's the start of forever."

CHAPTER 15
FRANCO

"I LIKE THE WAY THAT SOUNDS," I admit. "Too much."

Chloe crawls across the couch on her hands and knees. "Can we take 'too much' out of your vocabulary, please? I don't think there's any such thing as too much when it comes to this. To us."

I watch as she settles herself on her heels, the blanket falling down around her hips.

"I don't expect a proposal, Franco," she says. "I need to repay what I owe you. Get the shop back on its feet. If it's even possible. There's still a chance I can't bring in enough to keep the store."

"What will you do if that happens?" I ask.

I am not ready to hear her say she'll leave, but the more I admit to myself that I want this, that I want her, the more I realize I have to accept that none of this is in my control.

She could close Latterature and leave Star Falls. Or ask me to come with her. Things are getting even messier. I hate messy. I hate multitasking.

I've never been good at complexity.

Could I have sorted out the paperwork at the shop myself if I spent enough time and focus? Probably. But that's just not how I'm wired. I'm not good at solving puzzles, finding paperwork, and apparently, I'm not very good at navigating complicated feelings.

I like things simple, direct, honest.

Things with Chloe are anything but that. But a part of me wonders if I'm the one making things so messy.

"What are you thinking?" She reaches across my outstretched legs and cups my chin.

"You renewed the lease here?" I ask.

I'm not good with this many moving parts. My mind feels fuzzy, and my hands curl up in impatience. I don't know what the fuck has gotten into me. Maybe I'm the reason I've never been able to date anyone seriously.

Fucking and fun are simple.

Feelings, especially feelings like this, plans and thoughts about the future, I realize now, are not.

"I paid for the next month," she tells me. "I'll barely be home though."

"What do you mean?" I ask. "You're leaving? Going someplace?"

She nods and releases my chin. "I called my mom last night. She asked me to come home for a bit. She had some really good suggestions about the store, actually. I think I'm going to spend the next few weeks until I leave getting the shop redesigned. I'll have a grand reopening on Black Friday and see if I can start to turn a profit. So, between being at the bookstore and my mom's, I won't be home much."

That's a really smart idea. Main Street does a booming business for the holidays. Even the tattoo shop rolls out specials and giveaways. Foot traffic increases, and a lot of residents buy local to support their neighbors, as opposed to buying gifts online or driving into Cleveland to shop at the big malls.

"Will you be here for Thanksgiving?"

"I get back a few days before," she confirms, crawling over my legs. "But I'll be getting the shop ready for Black Friday. I think it's going to take more work than I even realize."

I spread my legs wide, and she settles between them, leaning her back against my chest.

"So here's what I think," she says. "I think you should help me name my dog." She lifts her face and looks at me over her shoulder. "I'm sure your mom will watch her while I go home for a few days. And since the shop will be closed the next few weeks, I'll be able to move furniture and do some reorganizing with a furry little companion to keep me company. Assuming my landlord says yes."

I like the sound of that. I like the sound of all of it. "If he doesn't, we'll sic my mother on him. Lucia doesn't take no for an answer, in case you hadn't noticed."

She laughs, and the sound is happy again. Free. "Come on. Let's think of dog names."

"Something tells me you've already thought of one," I say.

She nudges me in the ribs with her elbow. "What do you think I picked?"

I don't have the faintest idea, but I'm going to have fun guessing. "Cliterature," I say. "After two of your favorite things."

She gasps in shock but then bursts into hysterical giggles. "Rude," she says. "The clit should be one of your favorite things, not mine."

"Oh," I tell her, "it is. *Yours* is." I kiss the top of her hair and keep guessing. "Captain Saucy Pants McGoo?"

She lifts a brow at me and scowls. "Now you're being ridiculous. Cliterature was better."

I wrap my arms around her waist and rest my chin against the top of her hair. "So," I say, "tell me. What are you thinking about naming Mama Dog?"

"Well." She scoots her bottom even closer to my crotch, sending my dick a message it doesn't want to ignore. "I was thinking Mia."

"Feminine for mine in Italian?" I ask.

She nods slightly, my head bobbing with hers. "Kind of a perfect symbol for what I'm building here. Something that's mine. My choices. My dog. My protection. My new life."

I swallow against the sudden rush of emotion that clogs my throat worse than a plume of diesel exhaust to the face. It surprises me, but it shouldn't. Everything about Chloe is thoughtful and sweet. I clear my throat and rub at my nose. "That's beautiful. Perfect."

"You're beautiful," she says. "And perfect in my eyes. Well, maybe not perfect. But I like you a whole lot."

"Hey." I lift my chin from the top of her head and angle my neck so I can nuzzle her ear. "I like you a whole lot too," I whisper. "And I missed you last night."

She turns on the couch to face me. "I missed you too," she says. "Did we solve anything?"

"All of it," I tell her, leaning forward to hold her face with a hand. I stroke the plush lower lip with my thumb and look into her clear green eyes. "Welcome to Star Falls, baby," I say. "It looks like you've finally come home."

She blinks fast and grins before physically throwing her body against mine. And God, when we kiss... The feeling is exactly like coming home.

Before I know what she's doing, she's unbuttoning my jeans and urging me to lift my hips. She helps me shake off the denim and my boxer briefs. Once I'm stripped of my clothes, she settles herself between my thighs and caresses my legs with her fingertips while blowing hot kisses against my bare, hard shaft.

I'm so hot for her, I'm nearly shaking with desire.

No matter how complicated plans are, these feelings are simple, and I relish them.

Being with Chloe like this is like riding my motorcycle. Easy, free, the flight and the wind and the speed so intoxicating that everything else seems irrelevant.

My pulse thunders as I watch her kneel on the carpet so she can get a better angle on my erection. She flicks the tip of her tongue against the underside of my head, softening and flattening her tongue as she lavishes attention on my dick.

She strokes my sac, fingering the tight seam between them in the way that makes the air fly from my lungs. My legs are tight and loose at the same time, the tension in my sac drawing my balls tight as she finally takes my whole cock into her mouth.

She hums along my length, then uses one hand to add friction and pressure to the licks and kisses.

Sucking me in deep, she pauses to peek up at me, and my heart nearly shatters at how gorgeous she is. Her nipples are so hard, and the one that popped past the fabric of the tank before now knows the escape route, and it slips out again, begging for attention.

I reach down and twist the erect bud between my fingers, saying a silent prayer of thanks that she has such sensitive nipples. When I'm super close to coming, I shift my hips slightly and grab her hands.

"Get on," I demand. "Ride me, baby."

She leaves the tank top on but shimmies out of her panties. She looks at me, her lids heavy, her lips parted, and steps close enough to the couch that with the slightest bend of her knees, she'll be able to line up her pussy directly over my cock.

"Chloe," I growl. "What are you doing?"

"I have ideas," she says thoughtfully.

"You haven't had an idea yet that I didn't love."

She reaches over to my hand and moves it so my fingers are on my dick. "Hold, please," she says playfully. "I'll be right back."

I fist my dick and stroke it lightly to keep it hard, but unless she's gone for several minutes, I'm in no danger of losing my arousal. I watch her bare ass cheeks peek from beneath my tank as she trots into her bedroom. She's back in seconds, holding something behind her back.

"Franco," she says, a glimmer in her eye, "say hello to my now ex-boyfriend. We probably will keep, like, a friends-with-benefits situation, but for the most part, you're his replacement."

What she's holding in her hands sends a thrill of excitement through my body. At the same time, I'm curious and intrigued. "Hello, little man," I say, my voice husky with need. "You can go fuck yourself because Chloe's got me for that now."

She fiddles with the buttons on the matte purple silicone, and it starts to buzz softly as it vibrates on a low setting.

"This is for both of us."

I raise an eyebrow.

She stands in front of me and sticks the tip of the purple dick in her mouth. Okay, fuck. That's hot. Her eyes flutter closed, and she licks the toy, but not in a demonstrative way. This is utilitarian. She wets it with her mouth and then widens her legs and moves the toy beneath the hem of my tank. She holds up the hem so I can see her run the wet tip of the vibrator along her clit. She focuses her efforts and drops the hem so I can't see everything she's doing, but I can tell by the way her lips part and her eyelids struggle to stay open that she's pleasuring herself.

"I thought you said I put that asshole out of business," I grumble, but I'm definitely enjoying the show.

She smiles and pulls the thing away from her body, then kneels above my lap and lowers herself onto my dick. I slide deep in a single, slow, agonizingly blissful thrust. She's drenched and tight, and the pressure is so good, I want to claw at her ass and blast her name from my throat. But her mouth is over mine, and she's kissing and nipping at my lips, so I follow her lead. We kiss while I'm deep inside her, my fingers twisting her erect nipples until she's panting for release.

She's still got the toy in her hand, but now she pulls back from the kiss and centers the tip of the thing as close to her clit as she can get it. She leans forward, all of her weight against my chest, and works her hips so that she's riding my dick while the vibrator works its magic against her clit. It's between us, and I'm literally her fuck chair, which suits me just fine. I can feel the gentle vibrations of her toy through my abdomen, and while it's not exactly adding to my pleasure, it's making my girl so hot and so demanding, she ramps up her thrusts faster and harder. Her stunning thighs are working, every muscle tight as she writhes on my cock, and that makes me greedy for more.

I could fuck her forever. All night. Every day. As many times as she'll have me. But something that feels this good won't last forever. Fuck, it can't even last all night. The way she's moaning and whimpering, horny and hot and working herself into a frenzy on my cock, I'm going to blow before she does if she doesn't come soon.

I add a little fuel to her fire by curving my back so I can draw a nipple into my mouth. She widens her eyes at my interruption to her flow, but once she realizes I'm trying to help, her mouth makes a little O-shape, and she lowers her chest so I can draw a thick nipple all the way into my mouth. I grip her whole breast with a hand, working her bud into my mouth and sucking, slurping, taking out all my passion and fear and need on that poor bit of pink flesh. With my other hand, I smack as much of her ass cheek as I can, the satisfying contact not too hard, but enough to earn another gasp of pleasure from her.

She's ratcheting up the speed on the toy, and then I really feel everything. The way her inner walls tighten as she reaches her pinnacle. The way she floods my cock with her juices as she comes. The way her hands and legs and chest go weak and slump against me as she lets the climax rock her body head to toe. She screams my name, not a ladylike little murmur, but a full-throated, "Fuck, Franco!" and I realize I've never heard my sweet Chloe drop an f-bomb before.

As soon as she's coming, I let myself go, stop holding back my pleasure. Just as she is trembling through her orgasm, I'm coming inside her, hotter and harder than I think I've ever come. Burst after burst of absolute ecstasy comes over me, and my eyes are shut, my mouth open, and I'm grunting my baby's name.

"Fuck," I moan.

Like a rocket blasting through space and then gently drifting back to earth, I come back to myself in a slow, satisfied drift, smelling her, feeling her everywhere. On my lap, against my chest. Loose strands of her hair have caught in my mouth, and I can smell the potent scents of our sex in the air around us. I'm weak and damp and happy and drained.

I don't bother pulling out, and she stays collapsed against me, breathless and with a sheen of sweat coating her skin.

She's still gripping the vibrator in her hands, his dull buzz-buzz sound reminding me we're not entirely alone. I take the toy from her hands and fumble with it until the vibrating ceases. He's sticky with her juices, and as much as I want to taste her, I don't think I'm ready to stick a fake cock in my mouth. Someday. With her, I'd try just about anything.

"I thought that guy was fired," I mumble, almost too boneless to get the words out. "But maybe we should keep him on the bench. You know, for the occasional assist."

"I knew you'd be into kinky threesomes," she murmurs just as weakly against my shoulder.

"Kinky threesome…" I repeat. I stroke the damp hair away from her face and pull her to sitting with me on the couch. "You *are* my dream woman, Chloe."

CHAPTER 16
CHLOE

IT'S A BEAUTIFUL, cool morning, and after I left Easy Start, I had three texts from Lucia, asking if she could meet me at Latterature. I said yes, and Mia and I took off in my little sedan, which now has brand-new brakes, thanks to Franco and Jack.

When Lucia meets me outside the store, she has a little gift bag in her hands and a card that reads "Mia." I unlock the store while Lucia coos over Mia and strokes her head.

The dog and I are inseparable now.

Best decision ever.

She follows me through every step of the store, even coming between shelves to find me if I move out of her sight.

"Lucia," I say gently. "I've noticed you look a little different. I like it," I rush on, "but it's different. Not as bright?"

"It's my friend Carol," she says, rolling her eyes. "She's selling this makeup now out of her, well, it's not her home. She's moved in with her boyfriend and is selling makeup since she doesn't feel she can go back to work at Easy Start."

I nod. "Earl's been really generous letting me work in her place."

Lucia nods. "Earl's not a bad man, just, apparently, a terrible lover."

I cough a rough laugh into my hands. "Oh, okay. Wow." I don't think I'll ever be able to look at my boss the same way.

Our small talk is interrupted by a rough knock at the door, followed by Gracie waving at us through the glass.

"Hey, babe." She clasps me in a hug, all rushing and breathless as soon as I open the door. Her black hair is up in a messy bun today, and she's not wearing any makeup. "Do you have any coffee going? I way, way overslept and need a jolt of caffeine. I've got a customer in twenty minutes."

"I'll start some and bring it over," I promise.

She sighs and nods. "You're a lifesaver." Then she looks at Lucia. "Hey Ma, what's going on?"

Lucia flicks a glance at me. "I was just going to try to convince Chloe here to give Carol some work in the shop when she opens. The woman is trying to make a living selling makeup to all her friends. We're going to go broke if she doesn't find a real job soon."

Gracie wrinkles her nose. "Chloe, can you afford an employee? Aren't you working Carol's old job still?"

I nod. "And I don't know for sure that I'm even keeping the store," I admit quietly. It's the first time I've said anything remotely like that to anyone but Franco. "I'm hoping to have a strong showing on Black Friday when I'm back, but if not…" I shrug.

Gracie ponders this quietly for a second, but then she nods. "You know, babe, we cut our costs way down when we cut back inventory. You know the body jewelry we have up front?"

I nod, having no idea what costs a tattoo shop could have. Other than ink and advertising, I couldn't imagine.

"That jewelry is expensive, and if it doesn't sell, we're sitting on money that can't do anybody any good. When Echo started as the piercer and scheduler, we changed our policies. We keep a small supply of basic studs on hand, but if people want specialty stuff, they have to order it from our website. They buy it through us at a markup, and then we notify them when it comes in. The customer gets the jewelry they want, and we get a cut, but we're not out the expensive inventory costs waiting until someone decides they want a pink bedazzled belly ring."

"That makes a ton of sense," I say. "Are you thinking I have too many books?"

She shakes her head. "No. But what if you cut out all the food besides coffee and cookies? I can't imagine how much it costs to have chicken and bacon and all those ingredients on hand all the time. You have to have waste."

My mind starts spinning at the possibility. I love the idea of reducing the food we sell. It won't end the café part of the business. I can still make coffee and offer pastries or even fruit and nuts and other easy to sell nibbles. But cutting back the food service side of the business will reduce labor, energy costs. I'm shocked I didn't think of it myself. But I've been so focused on what I can afford to spend, I wasn't even thinking about what I might be able to save.

"As long as you promise to keep making me those peanut butter crisps," she warns, shaking a finger at me. "Got to run. This is for the coffee." She drops a crisp five on the counter before I can wave her away.

"Gracie, no." I try to stop her, but she's already out the door, her messy bun flopping wildly as she runs.

"Make the coffee. I'll bring it to her when it's done so you can work," Lucia says. "But first, open your gift."

I slide my finger under the flap of the envelope addressed to "Mia." Of course, the card is really for me. It's blank inside, but on the front is a glittery red heart that reminds me of something Lucia would pick out.

She's written a note inside wishing me a happy Thanksgiving and telling me how much she treasures having me in her life.

"Oh, Lucia," I say, tears stinging my eyes.

"There's more," she says, nodding toward the little gift bag.

I pull out the tissue paper, and inside is a gold necklace, just like the one she wears. The necklace has a gold heart with some writing engraved on it. I look closer and make out the words *bella vita* etched in a delicate font.

"What's this?" I ask. "Why are you giving this to me?"

"*Bella vita* means beautiful life," she explains. "I've had such a beautiful life, and I've done my best to give that to my kids." She holds up her hand as if to stop me from refusing or arguing. "I'm not getting ahead of myself, but I am counting on my son not to screw things up with you." She smiles. "No, seriously. When you go home, I imagine it's going to be very hard. Seeing your mom for the first time in so long. Being away from the pressures of the business. I just want you to know, sweetie, that you are loved. No matter where you go or what you do, you deserve a beautiful life."

She looks like she wants to say more but, instead, shuffles me into the kitchen. "Let's make my daughter some coffee, and I'll let you get to work."

"I'm so lucky to have met you, Lucia," I say, wrapping my arms around her. I really mean it.

She's been more of a mother to me than my own flesh and blood. Lucia has done everything in her power to bring me into the fold and make me feel at home in Star Falls.

Glancing around the shop as she hugs me back, I hope I can make it profitable, or else I don't know if Star Falls can stay part of my future.

When Mia and I arrive at Franco's, he's in the garage working on his bike. As soon as I open the car door, Mia bolts into the garage and plasters her paws on Franco's legs.

We've been working with her on basic commands, but jumping up and pawing people when she greets them is something she can't seem to stop doing. I can't blame her much. When I see Franco, I want to do the same thing. But with a lot fewer clothes on.

"Hey, babe," he calls to me. "You want to let her out back to run? I need a couple more minutes here."

"You got it, handsome." I open the door into the house and urge Mia through the living room, and let her out into the yard through the sliding glass doors.

I check to make sure there's nothing unusual out there for her to get hurt on, then I refill her outdoor dish with water.

"Play a little bit," I tell her like she's human. "I'll be back for you in a few."

I head back to the garage and lean against the wall, watching as Franco works. Times like this are when I feel most at peace. I love when we cook or walk the dog or hang with his family.

But when he's lost to his tinkering, grease on his hands, a bandanna holding the hair back from his eyes, he's so peaceful. There's no worry, no stress.

He's just a man whose brain is solving a problem or entertaining some interesting challenge on the bike he's trying to restore. I appreciate his intensity and his focus. Most of the time. I watch him and then grab a lawn chair, pull up a book on my phone and read, or make notes about the store.

But tonight, knowing I'm leaving in the morning and I'll be gone for days, I just want to be close to him. To hold him tight and smell the oil and smoke and salt of his skin.

I watch him for a few minutes until he turns and yanks the bandanna off his hair. The longish layers are flat, but he shakes his head, and they fly around his face, making me laugh. He wipes his hands on the bandanna before pressing the button to close the garage door. "You worried about going home?" he asks, giving me a quick kiss hello.

I shake my head, but in truth, I am a little apprehensive.

"What's this?" He strokes the charm around my neck and squints to read the engraving. "Ma gave you this?" he asks.

I nod. "She's such a sweetheart." I'm starting to get emotional. In a couple hours, I'll leave Mia and Franco and go back to my aunt's apartment alone. Tomorrow night, I'll go to sleep in my childhood bed at my mother's home. I'll be a world away, and yeah, I can't help wondering. Worrying.

"Shit," Franco grumbles. "Way to show me up, Ma. I haven't gotten you a single present yet. Now every time you feel that necklace, you're going to think of Lucia."

I shake my head. "No," is all I can say. "I'll be thinking of you every time. I wouldn't have you without her, remember."

"Let's not give her more credit than she's due," he says. He lifts my chin with a finger. "Can I give you a little something to remember me by?"

"What do you have in mind?" I ask, grinning.

He claims my lips in a tender kiss, soft and gentle. My eyes close and I breathe in the scent of him, feel the scrape of his stubbled chin against mine. He wraps his hands around my waist and holds me close, his tongue sweeping against mine. He tastes of cinnamon and a hint of sugar, like he was munching on mints while he worked. He's delicious and fiery, his kisses hot, and his hands on my hips tugging me close.

"You want me, baby?" he asks, his voice rough against my lips. He lowers his mouth to my neck and leaves scorching kisses from my jawline to my throat.

"God, yes." I lean into his hold, his already-hard cock pressing against the zipper of his jeans.

I move toward the door, but he takes my hand and shakes his head. "I want you here," he says.

"Here?" I echo. "In the garage?"

"I've been dreaming of bending you over my weight bench all day," he growls.

I'm more than willing. I'm so ready for whatever he has in mind. "How are we doing this? Am in your lap, am I…"

He holds up a finger. "You trust me, babe?"

I cock my chin, wondering exactly what he wants to do with me. To me. The uncertainty brings an immediate throb between my legs, and I'm already feeling myself grow wet with arousal. "Of course I trust you," I say. "Tell me where to throw my clothes."

He laughs and takes a seat on the workbench with his knees spread wide. "I'll tell you exactly what I want," he says. "Anything you don't like…"

"I'll tell you," I promise, licking my lips in anticipation. I tighten my legs, needing to rub my thighs together to ease the ache mounting in my core.

He leans back and just watches me. "Strip."

I immediately toe off my boots. As I wriggle out of my pants, I try to be sexy about it, but I end up shaking my bum and almost tripping onto the cushiony mat under my feet. "A little less stage-dive and a little more stripper," I mutter to myself.

He laughs, but he grows quiet as I shove my panties down and toss them away. I'm wearing a thick sweater with a puffer coat over it, which must look hilarious, but he's staring at me like I look good enough to eat. I stand there, bare from the waist down and dressed like a snowman on top.

"All of it," he says, lifting his chin.

I unzip my jacket and shrug out of it before taking off my top and my bra.

"Touch yourself. I want to watch you play with your nipple. Just one."

I do as he says.

I stare at him, swallowing hard as I twist the tip gently between my fingers. "Oh…" A little moan escapes me. When I touch my own breasts, it never feels as good as when he does it. But with him watching me, his hands on his thighs, his lips parted, I've never felt more wanton. My own touch brings me pleasure, and I try to give in to it, squeezing my nipple a little harder, twisting it a little farther.

He wiggles his fingers. "Come here. I want your ass in my face," he says.

I walk toward him, and when I reach the workout bench, I turn around again and face the garage door. My butt is facing him and is almost level with his face.

"Perfect," he whispers. "Now, spread your legs apart and touch your clit. I'm going to watch."

With my bottom facing him, I reach between my legs and slip two fingers through my trimmed hair. I'm already ridiculously wet, so I slide some moisture from my pussy and trace light circles over my clit.

My legs feel a little weak, and I don't know how long I can touch myself like this standing up.

"Did you like being spanked?" he asks.

"Yes." I lick my lips, loving the way it felt.

"Do I have your permission to do it again?"

I nod, not answering with words because I don't trust my voice. I want it. I want him. I want everything.

I swallow hard and cup my pussy. I feel his warm, rough palm stroke my backside, and then his hand is gone, only to return in a quick, firm slap.

The sound of his skin against mine is erotic and dirty, and the actual spank doesn't hurt at all. There's this delicious prickle against my skin.

"Good?" he murmurs, his breath hot against my thighs. I'm so close to him that when he breathes, the sensation of hot air then cool breaths sets every little hair on my body on alert.

My skin is deliciously awake, raw, and desperate for sensation. Any sensation. I whimper and obey when he reminds me, "Clit, baby. I want you to play with yourself while I play with you."

I stroke my clit and gasp as his palm bounces against my backside a second time, then a third.

"I'm not hurting you, am I?" he asks.

"God, no," I breathe. "But I'm not going to be able to stand much longer, Franco. My legs…"

He gets up off the bench then. "Hands on the bench and bend over. Ass up high."

I'm quick to move, eager to have his cock inside me. He moves my legs wider apart, and I nearly squeal in surprise when I feel his tongue sweep across my pussy. But the sound is stolen from my throat when he smacks my bottom again. My butt cheek is tender, the skin quivering, but his tongue at my seam and my fingers at my clit are making waves of intoxicating arousal flood my senses.

I can't think, can't speak words, can only coo and ooh and moan as his tongue softly invades my core while his hand works its magic against my bottom.

I hear the sound of his pants unzipping and feel him stand behind me, his hard thighs lining up with the back of my legs. "Hold on tight, baby."

I grip the workout bench for dear life and lift my hips so he can angle his cock between my legs. I'm so wet and so aroused, I see stars behind my eyelids when he thrusts deep.

He slides inside me, dragging his cock in and then out in such slow, agonizingly good strokes that I am begging, whimpering, and shoving my hips at him, desperate for more.

He cups my exposed left breast with one hand, tugging on the nipple that's already aching and raw. Then he rocks his length inside me, never fully withdrawing, but working his hips so fast that I am overcome with bliss.

I lift up on my toes so he can hit just the right angle, and with a few more pinches at my breast, I'm soaring, flying, screaming his name as a climax fires through my limbs.

Franco starts to come not long after I do, while I'm still bent over the workout bench, my bum in the air, and his hips resting against me.

He roars as he releases, both his hands now on my hips where he can hang on tight while he rides out his pleasure.

He places his mouth next to my ear, his breathing rushed and erratic. "A little something to remember me by while you're gone."

I smile to myself, knowing I'd never be able to forget.

CHAPTER 17
CHLOE

MY EYES FLY open to the sound of pounding on the front door. I turn my head, and Franco's still fast asleep at my side with a pillow thrown over his head.

I debate for a second on waking him up, but he more than outdid himself with the naked activities the evening before.

It's probably Lucia. It wouldn't be the first time she dropped by unannounced.

I grab my oversize sweater, covering my upper body and most of my legs. I can barely see, but somehow I make it to the front door without banging my elbows against the walls.

I don't look outside first. My mind is too out of sorts from sleeping. Instead, I pull open the door and come face-to-face with someone I don't know.

I blink, confused, and she does the same. She leans back, staring at me.

"Um," she mumbles before her eyes do a slow trail down my body. "Who are you?" Her voice is snotty, like somehow I don't belong at my boyfriend's house.

"I'm Chloe, Franco's girl." The words sound weird and foreign coming out of my mouth. We've had the talk, but I've never said them to anyone else before, and although it was strange to say, I liked how they sounded.

"His girl?" the woman repeats, her lip curling in disgust. "His girl?"

I nod as I peer over my shoulder and pull my sweater tighter around me, hoping Franco's not far behind. But he's not. There's no motion coming from anywhere. Just me and whoever the woman is who's currently looking at me like I don't belong where I am.

When I turn my head back around to look at the stranger, she's still staring at me, shaking her head and mumbling to herself.

"Can I help you?" I ask, trying to be polite.

She could be anyone. Maybe she's his cleaning woman. His house is impeccably clean, almost too clean for him to do it himself. Or maybe she's a relative because his family is too big for me to even wrap my mind around.

"Uh, yeah. I'm Franco's girl," she informs me as she crosses her arms, looking at me like I'm an intruder.

I blink and jerk my head back. "You're Franco's girl?" I ask, confused and wondering if I've been played.

Wait. There's no way the entire family is in on some

grand ruse for Franco to get into my pants. I've been with him for a while, and this woman has never showed up before. Lucia hasn't mentioned anyone else, and there's no way in hell she and Mario would welcome me with open arms if they thought Franco was involved with someone else.

The woman is beautiful. Stunning. Totally someone I could see him with, but the man is mine now. I don't care if I'm not his old type; I'm damn sure his new one.

"I'm sorry," I say to her, my voice saccharine sweet. "What's your name?"

It's not lost on me that I'm barely wearing any clothes as I stand in the doorway on full display for any of his neighbors to get quite a show. In a small town like this, someone's bound to be looking. I have no doubt that by later today, news will have traveled about my public indecency.

The brunette touches her chest. "I'm…"

"Olivia, what the hell are you doing here?" Franco asks from behind me.

I turn and glance at him over my shoulder. He's wearing nothing except a pair of sweatpants, and he's scrubbing his hand through his hair, making the messiness even worse but somehow looking hotter. It's so annoying.

"Franco," she says softly, her face immediately flushing as her eyes travel down his body like she did to me when I opened the door. But this time, it's hungry and less critical. "I was…"

Franco's hand slides around my waist, and he puts the weight of his arm on my hip. He bends his neck, peppering my jawline with a few light kisses. "Morning," he whispers against my skin as Olivia's words die in her throat.

"I was…" she repeats, but again doesn't finish.

"It must be important because you never drop by," he says to her, his entire body pressed against my backside, including his morning wood.

I do my best to seem unaffected, but this girl is trying to start shit with me when I've never done anything to her. "Olivia was just telling me she's your girl," I inform him, wanting to clue him in on our brief conversation before he decided to join us in the doorway.

"Liv," he says, his voice not as pissed as I was hoping. "Why do you have to lie?"

She shrugs with a devilish grin. "Life's too boring sometimes. And the look on her face." Olivia laughs, and it takes everything in me not to lift my hand and help wipe it off her face.

Breathe, Chloe.

"You've always been such an asshole," he tells her, which in the little time I've known her, I can say is totally true.

"I wouldn't be me unless I was stirring up some sort of trouble." She gives Franco the biggest smile before sticking her hand out to me. "I'm Olivia. I'm not Franco's, but the way you're dressed, I know you are. Way to go, girl," she says to me, waiting on me to take her hand.

I'm always cordial. It's one of my flaws. I have the inability to be rude on the outside, even if I'm thinking all the thoughts. "I'm Chloe."

She gives me a genuine smile. "It's nice to finally meet the woman I've heard so much about. You're the talk of the town."

"Olivia is one of Gracie's friends."

"Her oldest friend, and add best to that too," Olivia corrects him.

I can see it now. They have the same fashionable style, and Olivia, much like Gracie, is covered in tattoos.

"What do you want, Liv? You've never shown up at my place unannounced before."

Does that mean she shows up randomly, but calls first? She may be Gracie's oldest and best friend, but if I were a betting woman, I'd say she's more interested in warming Franco's bed than talking to his sister.

"My car's about to shit out on me, and I was driving by and thought I'd come straight to the source instead of trying to make it all the way to the shop." She pitches her thumb toward the sleek sports car parked in Franco's driveway. "Would you look at her? Please," she begs, batting her eyelashes at Franco.

He grunts, but there's no doubt about the way he'll answer. Franco's a good guy. He can't say no to anyone,

231

especially a family friend in need. "Give me a minute to get dressed, and I'll take a look."

"I have to go," I tell him, because I don't want to get on the road late, and I'd rather not be stuck in any type of rush-hour traffic. "Mom's waiting."

Franco presses his hand deeper against my waist. "You sure you can't stay a little longer?" he whispers in my ear. "I'll make it worth your while."

I want to stay and keep an eye on Olivia. I don't trust her, but I trust Franco and the connection we have…the history we've made in such a short amount of time. "I can't, honey. I'm sorry."

"Honey," he murmurs. "I like that."

"Can you move your car to the other side while I grab a shirt, Liv? Chloe needs to head out."

"Mom's house. Sounds like a fun afternoon," she says, fishing for details.

"It will be," I tell her, but I'm lying. I want to have high hopes for the time my mother and I are about to spend together, but I've learned those dreams are often quickly squashed, especially when she's involved.

"Maybe I'll see you around sometime," she says as she takes a step back.

"She owns the bookstore next to Gracie's," Franco tells her.

"Latterature?"

I nod. "That's me."

"Aww. You're related to Ms. Ann?"

I nod again. "She was my aunt."

For the first time, Olivia's face isn't filled with mischief. "I liked her. She was a nice lady. I spent a lot of afternoons after school in there."

I smile at her kind words. "Well, stop in again sometime," I tell her and want to kick myself for uttering those words.

"I may do that." She waves as she hustles back to her car.

"You okay?" Franco asks as I turn around, still caged by his arms and body.

"Fine." I smile, but it's not entirely real. I'm too nervous about heading home and agitated over Olivia's arrival and the way she made my stomach twist.

"Liar," he says with a chuckle.

"I have to go," I remind him as he tries to grope my ass. "And people are watching."

He lifts his head and looks around. "I see no one except Liv."

"That's enough." I push against him lightly, not angry or annoyed with him. "Save this for when I get back."

"This won't save." He presses his cock against me, and it takes all my willpower not to cave.

"It'll have to. I'm sure you'll survive. It's only a few days."

He pouts as he releases me, looking like a sad creature who was just denied something he wanted for Christmas but got a knockoff instead.

"That's like an eternity, baby." He reaches for me, trying to suck me in again.

"Olivia's waiting," I remind him, and her name is sour on my tongue. "But remember—" I reach down and grab his stiff cock "—this is mine and not hers."

His eyebrows rise. "I like this side of you."

I give his dick a squeeze before releasing him. "Don't you dare go outside without a shirt."

Franco laughs. "Because of Olivia?"

I twist my lips, pulling my sweater tighter against my front. "No."

"Lies," he whispers. "She's no one, baby."

"She wants to be someone."

He shakes his head. "What she wants and reality are two very different things."

"Not if she gets her way."

He may like this side of me, but I do not. I've never been the jealous type. I've also never been this deep with a man.

"I have the woman I want," Franco says, pulling me back against him before I make it too far. "Don't forget that either, Chloe. You're mine and only mine."

I melt into his touch, hating that I have to leave. "I'd never be able to forget it even if I wanted to."

Part of me hates the hold he and his family have over me so quickly. I've never met another group of people that make me feel like I belong like the Bianchis. It's terrifying that somehow it'll slip away, but I remind myself that Franco's in just as deep as me. This isn't a one-sided relationship.

I push my ass into him, thrusting myself toward the bedroom. I snag my leggings off the floor and start to shimmy into them before he has a chance to grab me again. Resisting him is damn near impossible for me, and I'm trying to put as many barriers between my body and his cock as I can. Luckily for me, it works this time.

"You sure you can't stay?" he asks, leaning against the doorjamb, watching me.

"I am. It's only a few days. I'll be back."

"Promise?" he asks.

"I'm not moving back to Pennsylvania."

"You sure?" he asks again.

"My life is here."

"With me?"

I nod, stalking toward him slowly. "With you," I say, lifting up on my tiptoes to kiss his lips. "Don't miss me too much while I'm gone."

"Impossible," he murmurs against my lips.

I close my eyes, breathing in his warmth and the scent that's uniquely him. "I'll text you."

"Not the same."

"Okay. I won't, then."

"No. No. Text me."

I laugh, kissing his lips one more time before making a beeline for the front door. I catch myself before opening the door and stick my bare feet into my boots.

"Bye!" I yell out, hoping like hell he's putting on more clothes before he heads out to help *Liv*.

"Bye, love!" he yells back to me.

I throw open the door, ignoring the curvy brunette who's on her phone as she leans against her flashy car, looking like something out of a mechanic porn magazine, if there is even such a thing.

"Bye, Chloe. It was nice to meet you."

"Yeah," I whisper. "Bye, Olivia." I do my best to be pleasant, even though I want to give her my middle finger.

As I'm pulling out, I see Franco stalking out of the house in the same gray sweatpants and a tight-as-hell tank top. It's a shirt, but not the one I'd feel comfortable with him wearing around a very hungry and inappropriate Olivia.

CHAPTER 18
FRANCO

IF CHLOE IS REMEMBERING me while she's away, she sure as shit has a funny way of showing it.

All day Sunday, I check my phone for messages or texts. So much so that both Earl, who's back from his fishing seclusion and managing the early stages of amicably filing for divorce from Carol, and Jack give me shit about it.

By Sunday night, I'm looking back at her texts, trying to read any little clue into what she's thinking or feeling.

I got a Saturday night text that said, "I made it." Followed by a "Miss you."

Monday is a repeat of Sunday. But worse.

So, I grump through all of Monday, checking my phone every five minutes and worrying that I'm a shit boyfriend. I've ruined myself being single and fucking

CHELLE BLISS

free all this time. Yeah, I've had no strings, no drama, but I've also got practice at the long game.

"Franco, you got a minute?" Earl's scratching his neck, a pair of reading glasses on his nose.

I nod and storm from the bay where I'm working over to Chloe's desk. It's hers now that Carol has filed for divorce officially and let Earl know she's not planning to come back to the shop.

"What's up?" I lift my chin at him and quickly take a look at my phone. Nothing. Again. No missed calls, no texts. Not even from my mother. That makes me realize that maybe someone else has heard from her. I'm thinking about asking Ma and Gracie if they've heard from her, but then that's going to start a whole thing that I'm not sure I'm ready to face either. I pocket my phone and look at Earl, who's got a stern look on his face.

"Son," he says, "in all the many years I've known you, I've seen you in a lot of moods. But this is one for the books. Can I ask what's going on? You're stomping around and cursing under your breath and obsessively checking your phone. Are you in some kind of trouble?"

I bark a rough laugh because, yeah, I suspect I probably am. Instead, I sigh again and shrug. "It's Chloe," I say. "Haven't heard much from her since she left for Pennsylvania."

Earl lifts his brows, white and bushy, one of them sprouting a single renegade hair that seems hell-bent on poking the man in his eye. "Oh?" he asks.

I haven't officially told anyone that Chloe and I are

seeing each other. Keeping my private life private is such a struggle. I definitely wasn't in any rush to share the fact that I'm seeing her at work.

But now, with Earl looking me over curiously, not saying something feels like a lie. "We've been seeing each other for a while now," I say. "So, not hearing from her while she's back home makes me think of all the shit I've done to make me seem like a real asshole boyfriend."

Earl nods, and I wonder if I've already said too much. "You feel like talking about it any?" he asks.

I don't, but I can't very well say nothing and confirm that I'm an asshole. "She tells me how she feels all the time. She's so affectionate and thoughtful, and my ma got her this beautiful necklace as a gift before she left. I feel like all I've done is..." I swallow the words "fuck her," because I've already said way too much.

He gets it, though, and shakes his head. "So, do you love her, son? Or is this a casual, sexual thing?"

"I...I am falling in love with her," I say. "It may seem to be too soon, I know, but—"

Earl holds up a hand. "Who says it's too soon? Go on. What else?"

"I've never dated anyone, not seriously like this. Never someone I'd see a future of more than a couple months with. We were dating two weeks, and my ma thought she was moving in to my place."

Earl's just nodding. Listening. Waiting.

"It's all just moving fast, and I don't like this feeling I get right here." I touch the middle of my chest, trying to push down the knot under my bones. "Maybe she's having second thoughts about me or about staying in Star Falls."

Earl takes in a deep breath and scratches his neck again. His hair is an ashy gray, the color of dirty snow, and he keeps it short. He's a man I've known all my life, and yet I realize I've never had a serious conversation with him. I've never asked how he's doing, losing his wife. His marriage of however many fucking years is ending, and I've never once given him a hug or asked if he's okay.

I suddenly realize it. That I've been hiding too. I may not wear bulky sweaters to cover my body, but I hide in plain sight. Behind a big personality and a pair of brass balls. If I'm always slick and hard to catch, no one will ever catch up to me. It's a great way to stay safe. Unhurt. Untouched.

I feel the opposite of that now. Raw. Vulnerable. Worried to distraction that Chloe is going to be done with me. I'm terrible at multitasking, and I feel like all I've done is worry since Sunday.

"I think, in relationships, we're each good at some things and not so good at others," Earl finally says. He claps a hand on my shoulder. "Son, when you love someone and you put their happiness before yours, you think about what you're not good at. And you try to be better. You won't always do it right. But if she loves you, she'll see you trying. And that will be more than enough."

I swallow against the knot of dryness in my throat. "That sounds like real good advice, Earl. Thank you."

"Do as I say, not as I've done," he adds. "As you know, Carol and I have split up."

That's far from news, but I let my boss say his piece.

"Carol wanted to work on things for years," he admits, pointing at his son, who's on his back working under a sports car. "Probably since before that one was even born. But I never managed to do anything right. Those aren't Carol's words. Those are mine. I only realize now that I've lost her, that the one person I really needed to be honest with and never was, was myself."

That hits hard.

"If someone really loves you, they're not going to judge you on your results. They'll judge you on your effort. You need to look inside, Franco, and decide what kind of partner you want to be to this girl. Woman, I'm sorry. I'm still old-school that way. Carol keeps telling me that's offensive. She's an adult woman."

I smile and nod. "No offense taken. I'm sure Chloe wouldn't mind."

"If you try and screw up, she can never say you didn't try. Women are smart, Franco. They see through bullshit and lies, but they also see the truth. Even when we pigheaded men can't admit it to ourselves."

He doesn't say anything more, and I truly get his

point. He's right. I have been doing what's easy and safe in this relationship.

Sex.

I'm great at it, and it bonds me to her, but is that really all I have to give? That, and a little money to make sure she had a phone. I don't even need to think about the answer to that. I would give her everything.

"Thank you, Earl," I say, and I mean it. I think he can tell. "Are you okay? I haven't even asked, but you've been going through a lot yourself these past couple months."

Earl nods slowly and then gives me a smile. "I am okay," he says. "Thanks for asking. I never imagined I'd be alone at this age, but I think it's been good for me. The soul-searching has been good, but the fishing's even better."

I crack a smile and turn to go back to work.

"Franco." Earl stops me before I get too far. "Why don't you take some time off? We're slow. Jack and I can handle the shop."

I cock my chin at him, wondering what he's getting at. "Are you sending me home?"

"No, not at all. You're welcome to stay, but Pennsylvania's not far away." He nods toward Chloe's desk. "I have her mom's phone number and address. Needed emergency contact information in case of emergency." Earl grabs a folder from inside Chloe's desk and scribbles a phone number and address on a sticky note.

"Happy Thanksgiving, son," he says, handing the paper to me. "I'll see you Monday."

I take the address and stare down at it. I freeze for just a second. Am I really going to do this? Am I going to surprise a woman I've been dating for just two months?

"Change your mind?" Earl asks, lowering those bushy brows at me.

"No," I say, throwing my arms around him and giving him a quick, hard hug. "Just wanted to say thanks."

Earl claps me back and nods, then starts shouting at Jack to turn his damn music down. I take off for my truck, a plan already in motion.

———

By the time I roll up to Chloe's mom's house, I'm a bundle of nerves. My thoughts have been everywhere while I drove here, and I almost turned around twice.

But I keep thinking about what Earl said. The people we love don't tally up our successes and failures. They only care that we try.

I've got Mia on a leash and a bouquet of flowers in my hand when I knock on the door. Chloe answers it, looking more than shocked. She looks like I've caught her, and she doesn't look happy to see me.

"Franco?" She yanks the door open and talks to me through the screen door. She fumbles with the lock on the screen and then shoves that open, nearly hitting me in the chest. "What are you doing here? Are you okay? Is your mom okay?"

This is the moment of truth. She's either going to be happy with my grand gesture, or she's not. I thrust the roses at her. "These are for your mom," I tell her. "I didn't want to show up at her home empty-handed."

"Thank you. Mom's not here right now. She's at work. You're freaking me out. What's wrong?" Mia is wagging her tail like crazy, and Chloe just now seems to realize that the dog is with me. "You brought Mia?" She drops to her knees and scratches the dog's ears.

Even though this isn't the reception I'd hoped for, I ask her if I can come in. "Can we talk?"

She nods and invites me in, and then she locks the doors behind me. Her mother's house is really tidy, decorated with dated but well-maintained tchotchkes and knickknacks on every surface. It reminds me a lot of Ann's apartment.

"Are you hungry?" she asks. "Thirsty? You must be."

I decline anything to eat or drink. My mouth is too dry and my stomach too unsettled. She doesn't seem happy. Definitely doesn't seem to appreciate my grand gesture. Fuck me. Listening to Earl was maybe a mistake? I don't know. I can't go back now, though. I'm here, so I'm going to tell her what I feel.

"Nothing's wrong," I tell her. "Nobody's sick, nothing bad happened back home. In Star Falls."

Her shoulders visibly sag, and I think she's relieved. "Oh, okay. Thank goodness. Then why are you here?"

I am still holding the bouquet of roses for Mrs. Harkin, so I drop them on the coffee table in front of us and just let her have it. "I'm an asshole, Chloe. When I didn't hear much from you after you left, I started panicking. Thinking of everything I've done wrong in the very short time I've been lucky enough to be with you. And I started thinking that maybe I've been treating you more like a fuck buddy than my girlfriend."

She's listening and nodding, her crystal-clear green eyes wide.

"I want that, Chloe. I don't know if I'm ready to live together full time, but I think you're going to have to push me. I'm set in my ways, but that doesn't mean I don't want to change. I want to change if that means I'm going to be better. Better for you."

I pause to take a breath and see if she's going to react at all.

"So, you drove all the way to Pennsylvania to tell me that?"

Mia is sniffing around curiously. I look from the dog to Chloe to my clenched hands. "Yeah," I admit. "I realized that I might lose you. And I couldn't let that happen without trying to show you how much you mean to me. Because you do, Chloe. I should have said it a thousand times a day, so you know. I'm falling in love with you. Fuck, I might be in love with you already." I know I am, but this doesn't feel like the way to tell her. Certainly not the time.

She worries that bottom lip between her teeth. "Franco, I don't know what to say. I can't believe you took off work. You drove all this way?"

I nod. "I couldn't wait another minute without saying those words to your face. I didn't want you sitting in your hometown, thinking about moving away from Star Falls, without knowing exactly how I feel. This shit's never happened to me before. I've never second-guessed shit, but here I am, wondering if you're second-guessing us."

When I say that, she crumples, and tears well up in her eyes. "Oh, Franco." She shakes her head. "You're already everything I want. I wasn't mad about anything. My visit here has just been hard."

"Hard? How? What's going on?" I'm immediately worried that something happened. "I'll take you home if you want to get out of here."

"No, it's not that," she says quietly. She chuckles. "It's so funny. All the years my mom sacrificed to put up with my dad and his bullshit. She's sure making up for lost time. I know she loves me, but she's been so busy with her friends that we haven't spent much time together. It's fine. I mean, I've had a lot of time to think and go through stuff. Mom gave me this." Chloe gets up and walks to her purse, which is sitting on the edge of the coffee table. She pulls out a check and shows me the amount.

"Three thousand dollars? Your mom is giving you three grand? What for?" I ask, folding it back up and handing it to her.

Chloe shrugs. "Mom was never able to have friends or her own money. She's living her best life now, and she wants to share some of what she can with me."

I wonder if this money means that Chloe has been thinking about not coming back to Star Falls. "A little cash must make coming home and leaving the robbery and all that behind you a lot more attractive," I say. I can't even look her in the eye. I don't think my heart can take it if she actually says she's been seriously considering not coming back.

But she shakes her head. "It's the opposite," she says. "I can't wait to get back. I've already spent all this money in my head. I figured I'd pay you back as much as I could first, and then after that…"

I stop her right there. "So, you're definitely coming back to Star Falls? And what about us?"

She shakes her head. "Franco, I've known from the moment I met you that you were the one."

"So, you're not mad that I'm here?" I ask. "Was it stupid to come?"

She shakes her head again. "It wasn't stupid," she giggles. "Babe, I'm in love with you. I want you and have since at least week two when I stole your tank top." She rolls her eyes. "I didn't really steal it, but I might have noticed that I scooped it up with my stuff when I was packing and just decided that tank would be happier with me."

I laugh but don't interrupt her.

"My mom wants to introduce me to her friends. They're all coming over tonight. Everybody is bringing something. I'm supposed to start the turkey in about an hour. Mom plans to work on the actual holiday."

"And I'm crashing the party. Fucking everything up," I fill in.

"You haven't fucked everything up," she teases. "But I'm putting you to work now."

"I'm all yours," I say, and I mean it.

CHAPTER 19
CHLOE

FRANCO LEFT BEFORE ME, needing to be at his parents' for Thanksgiving dinner. I needed time to prep the store for the big reveal and sale tomorrow.

Franco will be at his parents', and while I have an open invitation to crash their Thanksgiving, I decide to go check on my shop first.

I disarm the alarm as I enter and lock the front door behind me. The store is quiet, and I turn on a few lights. Sheets still cover the front glass so passersby can't see the decorations I've put up. But they look impressive after a few days away. I check the kitchen, and the cider, hot cocoa, and coffee are ready to be brewed. I'll be back here tomorrow at first light to get things started.

I'm just about to shut off the lights when there's a loud knock at the door. I shake my head. Surely none of the Main Street businesses are open on Thanksgiving?

"We're closed," I call out.

But the guy's persistent. "Can I use your bathroom?" he asks. "Sorry to ask, but every place is closed."

I look the guy over, alarm bells ringing every possible way in my head.

No, no, no.

I'm here alone, and he must know as much. I scan his face and don't recognize him, but I don't really know anyone in Star Falls, definitely not a lot of young guys.

He's smiling, but he seems a little flustered and impatient. "You coming?" he yells through the glass.

As I watch him shift from foot to foot in the cold, he jams his hands into his pockets and pulls them back out again. A black mask falls out of his jacket.

My heart catches hard in my chest. It can't be the same guy. It just can't.

He looks down and picks it up, then slides it over his hair.

My shoulders sink as I relax. It's not a black mask. It's a regular old cap.

But no matter what, I know I can't let this guy in. I'm alone. All of Main Street is deserted.

My heart is thundering hard, and I'm thinking fast. "One second," I call out, holding up a finger. "I left my keys in the kitchen. I'll grab them and unlock it."

I'm not sure if he could hear what I was saying over the shaking of my voice, but when I hold up a hand, he grins and nods, moving from shoe to shoe.

My keys are actually in the back pocket of my jeans,

but I tug my big sweater over my bottom so he can't see I'm lying. I head calmly back to the kitchen and give him a "just a second" gesture while I disappear into the back.

I grab my cell phone and dial the non-emergency number for the local police. The dispatcher answers on the first ring, and I explain there's a man casing my store and I would like an officer to drive by to make sure I get to my car okay.

The woman confirms there's a squad car nearby. She says to stay put in the store. The officers will knock on the front door when they arrive.

I am freaking out now, though. I've put something in motion that can't be undone. If the guy is just an innocent guy who needs a bathroom… But to be honest, I'm pretty sure that's a line of bullshit.

My nerves are frayed, and the few minutes it takes the cops to arrive feel like three hours. I'm panicked and pacing and don't know what to do when I finally hear a loud knock at the front door.

I peek out from the kitchen and see two uniformed officers standing there. Behind them, the lights are blaring, but there's no siren sound. I feel relief and fear at the same time, but since I don't see any sign of the guy who wanted the bathroom, I come out, cross the store, and unlock the door for the officers.

"Ma'am, are you okay?" the officer asks me.

"Yes, I'm fine," I say. "Is he still out there?"

The officer shakes his head. "We caught him."

My eyebrows rise at their speed. "Thank you."

He gives me a chin lift. "No thanks needed, ma'am. He'll be off to the station in a few. Another car got here before us and were able to chase him down. When they searched him, they found a large knife in his possession."

My stomach twists remembering that night and the knife he had. A knife he could've used on me. "Oh my," I whisper, trying to keep myself upright and the fear out of my mind.

He's been caught.

He'll never hurt you again.

"You saved a lot of businesses a lot of losses by calling," the officer assures me. "If you need anything else, please don't hesitate to call."

As soon as I close the door to the shop, I slide my back down the door, placing my ass on the floor. I give myself five minutes to have a freak-out before I compose myself and head out the door.

It's over. He's gone forever.

I arrive at the Bianchis empty-handed.

Franco's eyes meet mine, and he immediately drops the pan of stuffing on the table and rushes toward me. I'm standing in the front hallway with my coat and boots still on.

"What happened?" he starts, but I shake my head.

"Can we talk for a second in private?" I ask. I love and trust the Bianchis, but this is something I want to share only with him. I don't want the noise and attention. I just need him to know what I've been through. I just need my Franco.

"Absolutely, yes." He watches me with concern on his face. I hand him my coat to hang up while I slip off my boots, and immediately, people descend to greet us. Franco shoots me a quick look before parting the crowd like a champion. I'm so, so surprised and grateful. "We need a moment," he tells them, "alone."

Bev and Gracie groan, and loud laughter ensues as the family urges us to go downstairs for a few moments alone. I try to smile and wave as Franco takes me into the basement kitchen, where food is stacked up waiting to be carried to the table.

"Should we wait?" I ask, motioning to the trays piled high with baked sweet potatoes and toasted dinner rolls. "I don't want to mess up the meal."

"Everything can wait," he tells me. "All that matters is you."

He pulls me close, and for a moment, I just rest my head against his chest. I lock my arms around his waist and hug him hard. He's wearing a soft flannel shirt with a white T-shirt underneath, and his smell is both familiar and comforting. He kisses the top of my hair and rocks me lightly, just waiting.

Doesn't urge me. Doesn't rush me.

Above us, I can hear laughter and heavy footfalls as

guests and family walk around. The music is muted, but I hear the occasional barks from the dogs. When my pulse settles a bit and I feel a little calmer, I release him and look into his face, explaining in as few words as possible what happened tonight at the shop. Franco doesn't interrupt until I'm done talking.

"Are you okay?" he asks, his body tense and his expression tight.

I nod. "I'm oddly relieved. They know who the guy is now, so even if he gets out…"

"He's not getting out," Franco says, his voice low and angry. "I'm going to call the station tomorrow and talk to the detective who is handling your case. Maybe I can file assault charges against him. He did fight me out there on the street. We'll make sure he doesn't get out anytime soon, babe."

I nod against his chest. "I was planning to have time to stop home and throw together some cookies or something. I can't believe I came here empty-handed. I was just so shaken." I wave down at my casual traveling clothes. I'm wearing yoga pants over a loose, comfy sweater.

"None of that matters," he says. He leans back to look me in the face. "You're home. This is a come-as-you-are place. No cookies required. And I love that I can actually feel your ass in those pants," he teases, but he doesn't touch my bottom.

Instead, he kisses my forehead and touches his nose to mine.

"Can I kiss you now, babe? I need to know you're really okay." His intense blue eyes are staring, and I hear the basement door open. "But I missed the shit out of you and have been looking forward to those lips all day."

"Yo, asshole." Before he can bend his face to mine, Vito's voice echoes through the doorway and down into the basement. "You done making kissy faces yet? Pops wants the sweet potatoes."

"Fuckin' V." Franco groans and shakes his head. "Come on down, but you're going to get an eyeful."

He leans down and claims my lips, and I'm giggling as we smooch. Vito storms past dramatically, covering his eyes and making sick sounds.

"Ugh, you two." He grabs the sweet potatoes from the counter, and as he rushes past, he shoves his face close to ours. He makes another gagging sound and sticks out his tongue, then looks at me seriously. "Glad you're back, Chloe. Now get your asses upstairs. I'm fucking starving."

Vito shuffles upstairs wearing his trademark slippers with no socks, but he is wearing real pants and a flannel shirt for the holiday. He doesn't bother closing the basement door, and Franco groans and shouts after him, "Asshole!" Franco releases me and cups my face in his hands. "I'd like Gracie to know the guy was caught, but why don't I leave it to you to tell my family when you're ready to talk about what happened tonight. That okay with you?"

I nod.

That's perfect. I want to share the story, but I don't want it to be the talk of Thanksgiving. Once all the small talk and bickering are over, I'll find the right minute to tell the family.

Before we head upstairs, Franco stops me. "I picked up something for you on the road," he says. "It's nothing big. I actually got it at a truck stop. It's a piece of crap, I'm not going to lie. But I saw it, and I wanted to give you a little something. I'll replace it with something nicer and more sparkly someday soon."

"Franco, you didn't have to…" But he pulls the gift out of his pocket before I can protest. The small item is wrapped in a nearly sheer white plastic bag with the letters THANK YOU printed in red ink. It's tiny enough to fit in his jeans pocket. I can't imagine what he could have picked up on the road between my mom's house and Star Falls, but knowing that he got it at a stop on the road trip he made makes it all the more special. Not to mention, it's the first gift—other than a cell phone, a dog, and a heck of a lot of amazing orgasms—he's given me. I unwrap the bag and inside find a tiny charm attached to a plastic card. The charm is gold toned and is in the shape of a key.

"It's to go with the heart Ma gave you," he says. "I always want to be the man who unlocks your beautiful life. Or some shit," he chuckles. "I'm no poet or whatever. I don't really do words. But I love you, Chloe. I've never been more thankful that my mother is a meddling matchmaker."

I wipe away the tears of laughter and joy that collect around my eyes as I add the very meaningful charm to my necklace. "A few more of these and your mom's going to think I'm copying her style."

"Don't you dare," he teases. He kisses me again, this time longer. His lips linger on mine, soft and insistent, sweet and whispering promises.

"Yo, asshole." This time, the voice that beckons from the top of the stairs is Benny's. "What are you two doin' down there? Pops is ready to carve the bird."

"For fuck's sake," Franco sighs, but there's a smile on his face. "You ready?"

I take his hand and think over all the things that have come together in my life the last few weeks.

Am I ready? Heck, yeah. I've never been more ready. The timing, the place, and the people couldn't be more perfect.

A new love, a new life, a forever home.

"I'm ready," I say, lacing my fingers through his, excited about the future.

CHAPTER 20
FRANCO

THREE WEEKS *Later*

"What do you think?" I step back, taking in the new sign on the bookstore as Chloe stands next to me.

She throws her arms around me as she stares at the front window. "It's perfect. Absolutely perfect."

Those are the words I'd use to describe her and the way she's seamlessly fit into my world. "It's not too much?"

"Is there such a thing?"

I've learned that in the eyes of Chloe, Gracie, and my ma, there can never be too much of anything. When I started to design the sign, I gave them a few choices and they always selected the most colorful and loudest option. "It'll grab people's attention."

"That's the point, silly."

I kiss the top of Chloe's head, looking around the busy street. "Are you ready to close up?"

Chloe looks down the street, soaking in the large crowds trying to get their shopping done before they run out of time. "Maybe another hour."

"I'll stay, and then I'm taking you to Benny's for a late dinner."

"Perfect," she says to me before pushing herself away. "I'm starving."

"Me too," I tell her, but I'm not hungry for food.

She moves toward the door, but I grab the handle first, opening it for her. She doesn't say a word, but she looks up at me with a smile that I don't think could ever grow old.

Chloe heads to the register, and I find an empty chair tucked away across the store to relax in. I grab a book off a random shelf that's within arm's reach and crack it open. I pretend to read because sitting in a bookstore without doing anything may seem weird, and I'm not here to creep out the customers.

But when I make it beyond the first page, my phone vibrates, saving me.

Gracie: Do not buy me clothes for Christmas, assholes. Do you hear me?

I laugh as I read her message, remembering all the horrible outfits we've bought her over the years. She's impossible to buy for, and as she's gotten older, it's become worse.

Benito: What the hell do you want, then?

Vito: What's wrong with the clothes we bought for you last year? They were the latest fashion.

Gracie: Do I look like I shop at Mico's?

Benito: All stores have the same shit.

Me: I didn't get you clothes.

Thankfully, I had Chloe to help me find the perfect gifts for Gracie this year. Without her, I would've ended up buying her a new robe or other bullshit she'd probably have no use for. My brothers are easy, but when it comes to Gracie, my mind goes blank.

Vito: You don't count. You have Chloe to help.

Busted.

I glance up from my phone, watching Chloe as she chats with customers. She looks more alive than I've ever seen her. The store is filled with people, and that means money. She no longer seems worried about the future of the store, which is a relief.

Benito: I was going to get you perfume. Cool?

Gracie: What kind?

Benito: If I tell you, it won't be a surprise.

Gracie: If it's aerosol from a chain store, then it's garbage.

Benito: Didn't know you were so fancy.

Gracie: I've known you assholes my entire life, and all you can come up with are robes, pajamas, and crappy perfume.

Vito: You're kind of a picky bitch, sis.

Benito: Too bad she's not as picky with her men.

Gracie: Um, I've seen what you invite into your bed. I wouldn't talk about my choices in lovers, B.

I bite my lip to stop myself from laughing and

causing a scene inside the bookstore. Although it's busy, it's still too damn quiet.

Benito: They're all beautiful creatures in their own way.

Vito: How about a Mico's gift card?

Gracie: Don't be a dumbass.

Vito: Me or him?

Gracie: Both of you.

Vito: What about Franco?

Gracie: I know Chloe has my back.

I cringe a little, even though I'm pretty sure Chloe nailed every gift for Gracie.

Benito: Isn't it the thought that counts?

Gracie: Yeah, but I'm pretty sure Mico's and robes require no thought.

She has a point, but we do put thought into her gifts. We have entire threads of text messages, trying to figure out what to get her, but always come up blank. It's hard enough for one of us to come up with a solid idea, but for all three of us…it's impossible.

Vito: I still don't understand what the problem is with Mico's.

Gracie: They have beautiful clothes that never wrinkle, but I'm not ready for the Mico's chapter in my life.

Benito: What did you get me?

Gracie: Condoms.

Benito: Solid idea, but I hate using them.

Me: You're going to hate a screaming baby more.

Benito: I'm pretty damn sure I'm shooting blanks.

266

Me: You're willing to risk the chance?

Benito: Haven't knocked someone up yet.

That's my brother's dumbass logic. It hasn't happened yet, so he figures it never will. He's bright with some things but so goddamn dense with others.

Me: Well, that's a good way to look at it. You've gotten lucky so far, might as well try to keep the streak alive.

Gracie: Sounds like a beautiful way to become a father. Lord knows, you only bang the best.

Me: By best you mean anyone with breasts, then he does.

Gracie: Someday you're going to have a person show up on your doorstep, and you're going to find out your thoughts that you were sterile were all bullshit.

That sounds like my mother's dream come true. She'd be over the moon if grandkids popped up randomly and the family grew quickly.

Benito: Not happening. No one's told me they were pregnant.

Gracie: I'm sure they'd be more than excited to tell you the news after you discarded them like the half-eaten scraps in your restaurant.

Benito: I treat them all like queens, even if their reign is short.

Gracie: You're all pigs.

Me: Not me. Don't lump me in with those boneheads.

Gracie: You've changed your ways.

Me: I've never been like those two.

Benito: We're not monsters.

Vito: We're lovers.

Gracie: Whatever.

Me: B, I'm bringing Chloe over for dinner in a bit as soon as she closes up the store.

Benito: I'll make something special.

Me: Thanks, bro.

Gracie: I'm starving.

Vito: Me too.

Gracie: Why don't we all go?

I glance up at the ceiling, wanting a nice dinner alone with my girl. But I know Chloe, and she loves to be surrounded by my brothers and sister. It must be an only child thing because every chance she gets, she invites them over.

Me: Meet there at 9:30.

Gracie: Perfect. My last appointment cancelled.

Vito: Solid.

Benito: I'll go save a table.

Gracie: You'll eat with us?

Benito: You just spent five minutes beating me up, and you want me to sit down and have a civilized meal?

Gracie: I took years of your brotherly abuse and still talk to you. I think you can take a few text messages with the reality of your choices.

Vito: Babe, you gave as good as you got. I have some scars to prove it.

Gracie: I learned from the best.

Benito: I have to go prep our dinner.
Gracie: Nothing too greasy.
Benito: Picky.
Vito: See you in an hour.
Me: Bye.
Gracie: Later.
Benito: Peace.

———————

"This is Lexi," Benito says, walking up to the table with his hand against a new women's back.

"New flavor of the month," Gracie mutters under her breath into her glass of wine.

I give her a chin lift. "Hey."

"She's going to join us tonight," Benito informs us, pulling over a spare chair from another table.

This is new. He's never invited anyone to sit with us, not even his close friends.

"Cool," Vito says, barely looking up because he's too busy stuffing his face with the fresh baked bread. "The more, the merrier."

"It's nice to meet you, Lexi," Chloe says to her as she slides into the wood chair as elegantly as I've seen anyone do it before.

Gracie's staring at Lexi like she has two heads. "I'm just...this is different."

"Be nice, Grace," Vito tells her like she's a little kid about to make a scene.

"We're old friends," Lexi says to the table, but she can't take her eyes off my brother. "We haven't seen each other in years."

Surprisingly, Benito's staring at Lexi the exact same way. I never remember him talking about her, but by the look on his face, it was more than a fling. "It's been at least a decade. I can't believe you wandered in here tonight of all nights and to my restaurant."

"When I saw the name, I knew it was you. There's not too many Benito's in this part of the country." Lexi places her hand on his arm, and my brother does nothing to pull away. She turns to glance around the table at each of us. "I hope you don't mind me crashing your family dinner."

"Not at all," Gracie replies. "What brings you back to town, Lexi? I don't remember you from school."

"I didn't go to school here. I moved to Star Falls after college when I started working for a local advertising agency. I stayed a few years and then headed to California to work in Hollywood."

"No shit," Vito whispers. "That's pretty fucking cool. Meet any celebrities?"

Lexi laughs, but she nods. "They're everywhere out there. They blend in after a while, and you stop being so starstruck when you run into them."

"No way. I'd never get used to it," Vito says. "If I ran into a hot actress or two, I guarantee I'd at least get a date out of it. It wouldn't ever get old for me."

I roll my eyes. "They wouldn't want your ass."

He folds his hands together on the table. "They all want a piece of what I have."

"And that would be?" I raise an eyebrow. "They want a guy who lives in his parents' basement? What else do you have except the same bed you've been sleeping on since you were pissing the mattress?"

"You're a real douche," he says to me. "I have a lot to offer."

"You forgot about the stint with the stripper wife," Gracie adds like I could've forgotten that clusterfuck.

"No one gives dick like me." Vito's gaze swings to Lexi. "I don't mean to be so crude. My apologies."

My brother thinks his cock is the greatest thing he can give a woman. He also truly believes no one fucks better. The man is delusional and somehow really confident, honestly believing his own bullshit.

She covers her mouth, hiding her laughter. "No offense taken."

"How's the store? It looked swamped today." Gracie asks Chloe, ignoring Vito's conversation about his abilities.

"Busier than ever. I'm just hoping it stays that way after the holiday shopping season."

"Word will spread about the better selection of books. You've really outdone yourself with all the new changes."

Chloe smiles as she curls her fingers around mine underneath the table. "I'm trying. My aunt had a decent selection, but it was time to bring it into more current times and ride some trends."

"You own the bookstore in town?" Lexi asks Chloe.

"Yeah. It used to be my aunt's, but when she passed, she left it to me."

"She was a kind woman. I had many conversations with her when I lived here. I didn't have many friends, but she was always sweet and a good listener."

"Thank you," Chloe tells Lexi. "It seemed she touched a lot of lives."

Lexi gives Chloe a warm and genuine smile. "And now you're going to touch even more people. An entire new generation here in Star Falls."

I already know Lexi's too nice for my brother. She deserves someone better than him and his womanizing ways.

"They're exactly as you described them," Lexi says to Benito. "He told me so much about you all when we were younger, and when he said you were coming for dinner, I begged for him to allow me to stay."

"Lex, there was no begging involved. At least not this time." He winks at her, and there's a collective groan from everyone around the table.

Chloe leans over, bringing her mouth close to my ear. "I love this."

I turn my head, looking into her eyes. "What?"

"Your family."

"They're your family now too," I remind her. She's one of us now, whether she realizes it or not.

"What are you two whispering about over there?" Gracie asks, never wanting to be left out of a conversation, even a private one.

Chloe straightens again in her seat but keeps her hand in mine. "Nothing."

"She said she loves our family."

Gracie reaches over and touches Chloe's shoulder. "We're your family too."

"Babe," Vito says to Chloe, and the term doesn't bother me at all. "You're one of us now, even if you're too good."

"Too good?" Chloe laughs. "I'm not perfect."

Gracie snorts. "You're pretty damn close to Mother Teresa."

"Am not."

Vito leans forward, invested in this conversation. "Name one bad thing you've done in your life."

Chloe squirms in her chair but doesn't answer right away.

"See," Gracie says, waving her hand at Chloe. "She's a saint. I don't know how Franco got her, but he did."

"Magic cock," I tell her.

"I stole a pack of gum when I was a kid."

All eyes at the table turn toward Chloe.

"Babe, that's normal kid shit. I wouldn't call that bad," I say to my girl, loving that she's so completely innocent.

"Ever steal a car?" Vito asks Chloe.

273

"No," she says with her eyebrows knitted together. "You?"

Vito shrugs with a guilty look on his face. "I plead the fifth."

"Sweet Jesus," Chloe mutters. "That's so bad."

Vito chuckles.

"Excuse me," Benito says, sliding his chair back. "I better go check on our dinners before it gets too late."

"I'm starving," Gracie says, rubbing her stomach. "I thought the food would be on the table when we got here."

"Is Benito ever in a hurry or on time?" I ask.

"Some things never change," Lexi states with her chin resting on her knuckles as she keeps an eye on the kitchen where my brother disappeared.

"Especially when you're talking about Benito," Gracie mumbles against the rim of her wineglass.

"He's a good guy," Lexi says to Gracie. "He really is. I've known some really shitty ones, and your brother isn't. He can be incredibly sweet and caring."

"I love all my brothers," Gracie replies. "They all have their flaws, but I wouldn't change a thing about them."

I wish I could bottle up this moment forever. Not what's being said, but all of us being together. Time is fleeting and life is precious. I've spent most of my life not putting too much thought into my family and the people who surround me. But as time slowly ticks away, I know there will be fewer and fewer moments like this.

"Are you okay?" Chloe squeezes my hand.

I turn to her and smile. "I'm perfect. This is perfect."

She leans over and offers me her lips. Without hesitation, I take them, kissing her roughly.

"I love you," she whispers against my mouth.

"I love you too."

And I know, if my life ended in this moment, there is nothing more I would've wanted. I have the dream. A good family. A good woman and more love than one person could ever possibly deserve.

EPILOGUE

FRANCO

"MA." I lift my face toward the ceiling and take a deep breath.

The woman has been relentless lately. Not completely different from how she normally is, but she's been outdoing herself.

"The baby needs all the things," she explains to me.

"I think we have all the things," I tell her, waving my arms around the construction zone that will become the nursery.

Ma shakes her head and hooks her hand in the crook of my arm. "Franco, you have no idea how many things it requires to raise a child."

I peer down at her as she surveys her work, buying everything she can get her hands on—or at least it seems like it. "Did I have seventeen baby blankets?"

She glances up, her lips pursed. "I had more."

I shake my head, not believing a word of what she's saying. "No, you didn't."

"Uh, yeah, I did."

"If I had three baby blankets, I'd be shocked."

Pops walks into the nursery and whistles. "Someone's credit card is screaming," he teases, thinking I bought all this shit.

"Yeah, yours," I snap.

His eyes widen. "Lucia," he says, his voice filled with disbelief and warning. "You didn't do all this."

Her hand tightens on my arm, and her eyes narrow. If I were younger, that look would've had me quaking in my boots. "Mario, don't start with me. This is our first grandchild."

"That you know of," I grumble. We've all assumed Benny has at least one out there in the world since the guy sticks his dick in everything.

"Hush," she tells me in that mom tone. "You want our first grandchild to have the best of everything, right?"

Pops walks around the room, running his finger down the stack of blankets I'd just been complaining about. "Finer things, yes. All the things…no."

"There's still more to get," she tells him, ignoring his concerns, like she often does. "The baby will want for nothing."

"Literally," Pops adds. "But Lucia, darling, you need to stop. Wait until he or she is here. Babies grow. Their needs change as they get older. Save a little buying power for that time."

"I'll get more," she tells him.

We know she isn't going to listen. He's wasting his breath trying to rein in her spending. By the time the baby is born, I'll be shocked if he or she will even be able to fit in the room with all the things my mother drops off every few days.

"Pops, how many baby blankets did I have?"

He looks at me funny. "What do you mean?"

"Did I have five, six, or three? You know, this," I say, holding up a stack of perfectly folded fabric.

His gaze drops to the pile, and his eyebrows knit together. "How many are there?"

"Who the hell knows. It changes daily." I drop the stack back on the dresser from where I grabbed them. "Did I have this many?"

Pops shakes his head. "You had one, and when that wore out, we bought another. Lucia," Pops says, turning his head toward my mother. "Did you buy all those?"

Ma smiles nervously. "It needs to match their outfit," she explains, like somehow it makes sense when it damn well doesn't.

"And which one is baby-puke color? Because everything is going to be covered in it for months," he tells her, shaking his head. "And I mean everything."

"Remember when Franco threw up in your mouth?" Ma asks him, laughing. "I'll never forget the look on your face."

I cringe thinking about it. Puke has never bothered me, but having someone, even a tiny human, throw up in my mouth is a hard pass. "That's awful," I whisper.

Pops covers his mouth like he can still remember the taste. "I'll never forget it. I learned not to hold him over my head after he ate. Some lessons are harder than others."

"I'm putting that away in my memory bank. No holding the baby over my head after eating," I state to myself, hoping I'll make it a lasting impression.

"It's best if you don't hold the baby over your head any time, not just after eating. Babies sleep, eat, poop, and puke, and all of them at the worst times possible."

"You make it sound like a great experience," I tease him.

"Best thing I've ever done. There's nothing like being a father."

My mother clears her throat.

Dad smiles at her as he mindlessly runs his finger across the top of the blankets. "Besides marrying my beautiful bride, of course."

"Smart man," Ma mutters under her breath before reaching up a hand to touch my face. "You're going to be a great dad."

"I had great parents. You two taught me everything I know."

"Then you're doomed," Gracie says, coming into the room with a cup of coffee in her hand. "We're all screwed up."

"Speak for yourself," I tell her. "Name me a normal person."

She moves her head from side to side like she's thinking, but we both know there's no answer. Normalcy is a falsehood. Everyone has issues, but some people have more than others.

"I'm kidding," she adds, bumping my dad with her shoulder. "We had the best parents."

"Had?" Pops asks. "We're still here."

"Yeah, but I'm grown."

"And still need a parent," Ma adds. "Where would Franco be if it weren't for me meddling in his life?"

I sigh. She has a point, but not one I like to give in to. She'll use it as an excuse to keep going on her butting-in, and that's the last thing I want her to do. "You did good, Ma, but it doesn't always work out."

Ma touches her chest with her fingertips, lowering her chin. "I know my children and what's best for them."

"We're not children anymore, Ma," Gracie explains like it will make a damn bit of difference.

"You'll always be my children. I don't care if you're eighty years old and using a cane. Always my babies," she repeats.

Gracie rolls her eyes. "Pops, you need to keep her busy so she doesn't butt into our lives."

Pops raises his hands and lifts his eyebrows. "I can only do so much. I'm just one man."

Gracie grunts into her coffee cup. "Bullshit."

Chloe waddles into the nursery, rubbing her belly. "I'm ready for this to be over," she grumbles. "Soon, my ass won't fit through a doorway."

I move away from my mother's side and slide toward my wife. "Gives me so much more to love," I whisper into her ear and touch her ass, which I've grown to love more than her flatter and less-full version. "We need to keep it."

Chloe looks at me with a horrified expression. "It's going. As soon as I can work out, it'll be disappearing."

"Shit never gets back to where it was," Ma tells her, ruining all Chloe's hopes and dreams of getting her pre-baby body back.

"Great," Chloe groans. "I could do without the extra padding."

I smile down at my girl. "It's the best part."

She slaps my chest with the back of her hand. "Shut up."

"Your tits and ass are primo," Gracie tells Chloe with a wink. "You get stares coming and going."

Chloe's shoulders slump forward. "It's hard to miss me."

I place my fingers under Chloe's chin, raising her eyes to mine. "You're the most beautiful woman I've ever laid eyes on."

She sighs. "Oh, okay."

"Babe, you're stunning."

Chloe grumbles.

"You're growing a life inside you. If we have a little girl, I want her to look like you and not me because let's face it, I'd make one hell of an ugly woman."

"Amen to that," Gracie says with a hint of laughter. "I tried to doll you up when we were kids, but nope, still ugly as hell."

Ma bursts into a fit of laughter. "Your brothers had patience then. They let you practice on them for hours."

Chloe's face brightens. "You put makeup on them all?" she asks Gracie.

"Yep. All of them." Gracie beams with pride, but I feel nothing except annoyance.

I hated when my sister would do our hair, of which we had very little, and makeup. She was so slow, and the shit was hard as hell to get off too. But I did it to make her happy, even if it was only for a little while.

"I want that for our baby."

"Then you better work on another as soon as you have this one," Ma explains with the biggest smile. "You don't want them too far apart in age."

"You know, I did it most of the time just to annoy the shit out of you guys," Gracie tells me.

"It worked," I mumble.

"I'm going to need a little time in between," Chloe says to my mother.

"Don't wait too long. It's better when they're closer together in age."

"More expensive, too," I say.

"It's not cheaper to have kids far apart. They're expensive no matter what, kiddo," Pops says. "I'd be rich if it weren't for you four."

"Rich in the bank, but poor in life and love," Mom tells him.

"Yeah, that too," he says, but I'm not convinced he thinks or feels the same.

"There's no amount of money I'd take to replace my time with you kids," Pops says. "You'll see, son. You'll give that child your last cent to see a smile on their face."

"Speaking of their… Do we know if we're having a boy or a girl?" Ma asks.

"We?" Gracie laughs. "Are you going to be in there pushing too, Ma?"

Ma waves her hand to Gracie to shush. "Do we?"

Chloe looks up at me and raises an eyebrow. We've known for weeks but have been keeping it a secret. Not an easy one to keep either. But we know once they know, the entire town will know. Not that it's a bad thing, but it's been nice to have a secret all to ourselves.

"We do," Chloe says softly as she looks me in the eye, waiting to see if I'll react.

I'm fine with them knowing. "Maybe Ma will stop buying yellow shit if we tell her."

"There's nothing wrong with yellow," Ma informs us like we're monsters. "It's a lovely color. Mint green, too."

284

"I agree," Chloe says, squeezing my arm. "Maybe we should let it be a surprise."

"No. No. No. No," my mother chants, shaking her head. "I want to know. I *need* to know."

"Don't make her beg any longer, son," Pops pleads with me.

"Fine. Fine," I say, looking down at my wife. "Do you want to tell her, or should I?"

"Jesus," Ma mutters. "Just spit it out. You're killing me here."

"You do it," I tell Chloe.

Chloe's smile widens as she gazes up at me. "Buy all the pink things," she says to me, but she's talking to my parents.

Ma gasps. "A girl? We're having a girl?" She squeals so loud I swear one of my eardrums bursts, and she runs to my father, throwing her arms around him. "Did you hear that, Mario? We're having a baby girl."

I wrap my arms around Chloe, holding her tight while my mother has her excitement-induced meltdown. I knew she'd be happy. Hell, I was over the moon to be having a little girl.

"Little girls are so special," Pops says to me. "You're in for a world of hurt and happiness."

"Pops, did I hurt you?" Gracie asks him.

"You grew up, sweetheart," he tells her plainly.

Gracie walks up to my father, throwing her arms around him on the opposite side as my mother. "I'll always be your little girl."

"That'll be us someday," Chloe says, clinging to me. "Our own little family."

I lean over, kissing the top of her head. "Just the three of us."

She peers up, placing her hand on my chest over my heart, giving me the sweetest smile. "Maybe four."

I could never break her heart or disappoint her. Family is important to me, but it's always been a dream for Chloe. "However many you want, baby."

She lifts a hopeful eyebrow. "Ten?"

I laugh, shaking my head. "Now you're getting extreme."

"You said however many I want."

"Let's start with one, and we'll see what happens from there."

"Deal," she breathes into my shirt as she holds me tight.

"Now, about the baby shower," Ma says. Thankfully, she didn't hear our conversation or else she'd be giving her input into how many kids she'd want us to have.

"I love you," Chloe whispers to me as my mother goes on and on about the party.

"I love you too," I say back, knowing my life will never be the same and hopeful for everything that's still to come.

The family is waiting… Gracie's about to be knocked right out of her boots and into the arms of someone tall, dark, and totally handsome. Don't miss out on this hot and steamy read. **Tap here preorder your copy of Never Too Soon now** or visit menofinked.com/nts

Turn the page to learn about the special bonus chapter!

Dear Reader,

I love Chloe & Franco so much I had to write a little something extra to their story. If you'd like a little more click the link below to signup for my newsletter and you'll get an **EXCLUSIVE BONUS CHAPTER!**

<u>GET THE BONUS CHAPTER HERE</u>
or visit menofinked.com/ntl_bonus

Gracie's story is coming next and she's about to be swept off her feet by a hot single dad. Preorder your copy of **Never Too Soon** and be ready to swoon!

Do you want to have your very own SIGNED paperbacks on your bookshelf? Tap here to check out Chelle Bliss Romance or visit chelleblissromance.com and stock up on paperbacks, Inked gear, and other book worm merchandise!

FREE EBOOK DOWNLOAD!

Looking for your next FAVORITE read?

Download **FLAME for FREE** and dive in. The family is waiting...

TAP HERE TO DOWNLOAD or visit *menofinked. com/flame* to grab your copy.

READ THE OPEN ROAD SERIES

Book 1 - Broken Sparrow (Morris)
Book 2 - Broken Dove (Leo)
Book 3 - Broken Wings (Crow)

WANT SIGNED PAPERBACKS?

ABOUT THE AUTHOR

I'm a full-time writer, time-waster extraordinaire, social media addict, coffee fiend, and ex-history teacher. *To learn more about my books, please visit menofinked.com.*

Want to stay up-to-date on the newest
Men of Inked release and more?
Join my newsletter at *menofinked.com/news*

Join over 10,000 readers on Facebook in Chelle Bliss Books private reader group and talk books and all things reading. Come be part of the family!

Where to Follow Me:

facebook.com/authorchellebliss1

instagram.com/authorchellebliss

bookbub.com/authors/chelle-bliss

goodreads.com/chellebliss

tiktok.com/@chelleblissauthor

amazon.com/author/chellebliss

twitter.com/ChelleBliss1

pinterest.com/chellebliss10